Beyond Forever

Beyond Forever

Cristina Monro

PARTRIDGE

Print information available on the last page.

To order additional copies of this book, contact
Toll Free 800 101 2657 (Singapore)
Toll Free 1 800 81 7340 (Malaysia)
orders.singapore@partridgepublishing.com

www.partridgepublishing.com/singapore

"No measure of time is enough. Let's start with forever" – **Edward Cullen from "Twilight"**

Other Books by Cristina Monro

Differences
Sibling War

For the living members of the
Montalván-Aguado Family
– all four generations

CONTENTS

PART 3
Blessings

PART 1

Soul Mates

Forever defies time within human boundaries. It depicts man's fathomless measure of eternity when it comes to relationships, where the overpowering emotions transcend time itself. In the realm of Love, there is such a thing as Forever.

Chapter

1

I had mixed feelings as I turned 60 on my birthday. It was not exactly a feel-good birthday, knowing it signaled seniorhood, but somehow it ushered in a sense of fulfillment and unexplained freedom. I awakened to the reality that I could be myself at this age, and I did not have to please anybody.

I had always been a free spirit. That is the compelling reason I never married. I used to be happy being alone. The veiled excuse was really because I had not fallen in love with any male. I happen to be a heterosexual woman who admires good-looking men, and I do not even have a lofty standard to follow. My friends regard me as good-looking too, and I believe I had my fair share of sex appeal, judging from the five or so gentlemen who courted and pursued me persistently. I have maintained my slim figure so far. Yet, no one has made my heart flutter, and I vowed I would marry only for love.

My life was never synonymous with boredom because I had tons of activities to fulfill. With my Church duties, charity work, weekly lunches with friends and former classmates, my painting sessions, exercising, regular reading, trying new recipes and crafts, and watching movies by myself, they left me no time to mope on singlehood.

I had since retired from the corporate world as an executive after 35 years of service, and the hefty retirement fund I received was more than enough to take care of me for my entire life, plus my sizeable share in the family estate. I may be considered "rich" by Philippine yardstick, but then the peso has meager value elsewhere in the world. My possessions are purely mine because I have no children, so I have no heirs to take care of in the day-to-day scenario.

When a woman opts to remain single, she is often questioned why. This is then followed by the statement, "It's a pity because you're pretty." There's no existing rule that says only the ugly ones are relegated to the single state. I find myself in an awkward situation when I am asked, so I just usually retort, "Why complicate my life?" and that shuts the person off.

I am not literally totally alone. I also have a sibling, nephews, nieces, uncles, and aunts, whom I see occasionally. My life got altered a bit when I acquired a dog rescued from the pound. She was a female mongrel with a beige coat. She was somewhat of a *mestiza* dog, perhaps of mixed breed, and I named her Khaleesi after the female character in "Game of Thrones". It was my first time to own a dog in my adulthood. I was compelled to adopt her from P.A.W.S. because she exhibited a pitiful expression. After having her neutered by my nephew vet Rafael, and groomed in a pet salon, she blossomed into an attractive animal.

When I was a small girl, I had pets too. Khaleesi was a lovable animal that kept me company. I did not allow her to sleep with me on my bed like other pet owners do. I love animals, and I believe they should have their own place to sleep, but she would snuggle with me on the sofa while I watched TV. She was a bit of an introvert and was not easily friendly towards people, maybe because she was somewhat wary, having spent time in a dog pound. Khaleesi is an important contributor to my life story.

During afternoons when it was not raining, and I was done with what I was doing, I used to put Khaleesi on a leash and I took her for a walk at the park in Makati City's Legaspi Village close to my one-room condo. It was normally a leisurely walk, which happened to be an extension of my regular 30-minute walk, to exercise her. I usually wore plain shorts, T-shirt, and sneakers.

On this particular Wednesday, we were walking along a tree-lined path with benches when Khaleesi suddenly increased her speed and made me race with her. She stopped at a maturish attractive gentleman with a well-trimmed light beard and mustache seated on a bench. She rested her front paws on him, and befriended him with her tail wagging as if she was familiar with him. She is not in the habit of doing this. The gentleman smiled and patted her head.

"Hi there," he said. He had a deep voice, decently dressed, and he looked distinguished with a mop of salt-and-pepper hair, more pepper.

"I'm very sorry, sir, for disturbing you. She doesn't usually do this with strangers," I apologized profusely.

"That's all right, she's just being friendly." I detected his British accent, which I found appealing.

"She's really not a friendly dog, so I don't understand why she's doing this. Again, I'm sorry."

"Don't be. What's her name?"

"Her name is Khaleesi."

"Oh, after the mother of dragons." I was surprised that he knew the name.

"We really have to get going." I had to practically pull Khaleesi away from the stranger.

"Goodbye, Khaleesi," the man remarked, standing up and patting Khaleesi again with a smile.

Khaleesi rewarded him with a friendly bark. I glanced at the guy and noticed that he was looking at me with an amused expression on his face. I found Khaleesi's unusual behavior embarrassing on my part. I usually talk to Khaleesi when we are by ourselves. Afterwards, I cautioned her not to bother strangers in the park. She looked at me directly and cocked her head in a quizzical manner.

After that awkward incident, I decided to avoid that particular park the next day for fear I might run into the same stranger, and Khaleesi would put me in a spot again. It baffled me why she easily warmed up to that stranger. He could not have been her former owner, otherwise he would have said so.

There are only a few remaining parks in Makati since large areas had been transformed into mushrooming condos, so I was forced to walk Khaleesi for the meantime along the side streets of Makati, like Legaspi and Salcedo, where there was ongoing traffic, by using the sidewalk.

After a day of taking an alternate route, I decided to walk Khaleesi again in the former park. It is actually more convenient for me, and there is no traffic to contend with. Thankfully, the stranger in question was no longer in the area, but I could sense Khaleesi was looking for him by the way she was walking in circles as if in search of something or somebody. I felt relieved that we could continue to walk freely without running into anybody.

Chapter

2

My best friend in High School and College is Sofia de Villa. The two of us come from the south, and we were both sent to boarding school by our parents. We became roommates. After College, Sofia went to Italy and met a guy there whom she eventually married. Her wedding was somewhere in Europe, and I could not attend it because I had just been hired by a huge corporation. She wanted me to be her maid-of-honor. They lived in Europe for several years until recently when her husband, Matteo Rosetti, was assigned by his company to head its office in the Philippines. We renewed our friendship and continued to see each other. She never questions me why I never married because she can see that I am happy in my state of life.

When we did not see each other, Sofia and I talked on the phone practically every day. One fine day, she called to casually ask me if I still do editing work. I worked as an Editor during my corporate days. I told her that occasionally I am asked to do editing, which I still enjoy doing. She said that a good friend of Matteo from his country needs an Editor to help polish his life story. He is passing through the Philippines during his Asian trip, and Matteo happened to mention to him that he knows of an excellent Editor.

"Was Matteo referring to me?" I asked, unsure.

"Yes, you. I told Matteo how good an Editor you are, and that you won several awards," Sofia replied.

"Thanks for your faith in me."

"Well, are you interested to take on this job?"

"Why not? It's challenging. This person must have an interesting life."

"I can assure you that he does. I can't tell you much, but Matteo can tell you more."

Matteo said that he's a good man and you'll like working with him. Are you free for dinner tonight? I'll prepare one at the condo where we can discuss it." The Rosettis reside in one of Ayala's plush condominium buildings in the heart of Makati.

"Okay, I'll be there. Sevenish? I suppose that's casual attire."

"As casual as you want to be. There'll just be the four of us."

* * *

I changed into a long-sleeved ruffled white blouse, paired it with a printed short skirt, and put on wedged black shoes. It was not too casual and it was safely decent enough. As I grow older, I shun high heels because they are very uncomfortable. I label them as "torture shoes". I can get away with flats because I am considered tall at 5'7" in my country.

I maneuvered my Prius into the building's parking space for visitors. A guard accompanied me to the elevator to get into the Rosetti condo. They are strict with security. It was 10 minutes before 7:00 p.m., and I am always prompt with my appointments. Sofia opened the door and gave me a hug. I spotted Matteo a few paces away talking to a tall gentleman, definitely more than six feet tall, with his back towards us. Then Matteo shifted his attention to me.

"Hi, Marianne. How are you? You look lovely. I want you to meet an important person who needs your assistance." Then he guided me towards their guest. "Your Majesty, this is Marianne Diez, Sofia's closest friend who is a topnotch Editor."

The person I found myself facing was the very gentleman at the park. I was rendered speechless for a second and just stared at him, and he sensed my discomfort. Up close, I noticed his unusual eyes. They were deep blue. He gave me a smile, revealing a good set of teeth.

"Hello, Miss Diez," the gentleman said with a welcoming smile, giving me a firm handshake. "I'm Franco. I'm pleased to meet you again. How's Khaleesi?"

"Khaleesi is just fine, sir."

"Have you two met before?" Matteo had a surprised look and became curious.

"Well, just recently at the park when Khaleesi suddenly became friendly with him."

"Did I hear Matteo say 'Your Majesty'?, I whispered to Sofia. She reacted with a nod.

"Gentlemen, I believe Marianne has a right to know who our guest is if they're going to be working together," Sofia suggested. "First, let's sit down to dinner and discuss it during our meal." Sofia and I were seated next to each other, with the men facing us.

As we start our meal after prayer, Matteo began, "Marianne, this distinguished gentleman is the reigning monarch of Marvella, a small island Kingdom ensconced near the tip of Italy facing the Tyrrhenian Sea. You may not have heard of it. I happen to be a citizen of this country, so he's my rightful King."

"All this time, I thought you're Italian, Matteo," I quipped.

"I'm actually a Marvellan. 'Marvella' means 'a miracle to marvel at, something extraordinary', and it truly deserves its name. It's a self-sustaining Catholic modern-day absolute monarchy, which is among the few in existence. Our visitor here is the 5th generation monarch. The size of the Kingdom is just around 500 square kilometers, and its population is about 2.5 million. You can regard it as a low-key monarchy, and His Majesty here is in the country *incognito*. We must be the only ones who know that we have royalty in our midst."

Matteo's statement elicited a collective laugh from us. The entire time that Matteo was speaking, the monarch's striking deep-blue eyes were fixed on me, as if gauging my reaction, and I could not help feeling a bit uncomfortable.

"His Majesty can elaborate on his project," Matteo said, turning to the gentleman next to him.

"Miss Diez," the King started in his impressive deep voice.

"Please call me Marianne," I butted in.

"Okay, Marianne. I am writing a book about our Kingdom, Marvella, its history and monarchy, and I need a good Editor who will go through my manuscript. You are highly recommended. None of my predecessors considered doing this, so I'm taking on this major project. I'm passionate about this because I want all Marvellans to be in-the-know about their Kingdom and its rich heritage. I will be here for the next two days. If you're free, we can meet during these days to discuss the project further. I'm staying at the Raffles Hotel, and I can reserve a private room for us on the ground floor if that's convenient for you."

"I live within walking distance to Raffles, so that's all right."

"Thereafter, we can communicate on Face Time, and I can e-mail you pages of the manuscript that I've finished writing. We can start tomorrow if you're free. How does that sound to you?"

"Perfectly fine. What time do you want me to go there tomorrow?"

"We can be flexible about time. It's really up to you. Is 9:00 a.m. convenient for you?"

"I'm okay with it."

"I'll leave word at the desk for you on where to go."

"Thanks." We continued with dinner, and I enjoyed the food Sofia prepared for us, especially the ice cream dessert because I love ice cream, and Sofia knows this.

"Marianne loves ice cream," Sofia disclosed.

"Is that right? You'll love Marvella because one of its major industries is dairy, and it produces the best ice cream in the world," Matteo remarked. The King smiled in agreement.

"I love ice cream myself, but I try to have the kind with less fat for health reasons," the King shared.

"Your Majesty, you're very trim, and you can still eat all the ice cream you want," Sofia countered.

"Well, I take care of myself. I exercise regularly and visit the gym. I have an enormous responsibility to take care of in Marvella, so I have to stay fit."

He really had a trim physique for his age. I probed Sofia privately as the men separated from us after dinner.

"How old is he? He moves like a young person without any trace of aging."

"According to Matteo, he's 64, but he seems strong and doesn't look his age. In Marvella, the King is king for life. When he dies, that's when his heir takes over, unlike in other monarchies where the reigning monarch can step down by choice. In Marvella, kingship is a lifetime commitment, and this King serves his Kingdom well, and takes on his responsibilities seriously."

"Does he have a Queen?"

"He has been a widower for 10 years now, so he has been without a queen for some time. He has a son and a daughter, and his son is his direct successor."

"The subject of royalty is so fascinating."

"I agree. Good luck on this job, Marianne."

"I'm really challenged, and that should be good."

"He's such a handsome monarch, don't you think? Just your type."

"What are you insinuating, Sofia? You are aware that I'm not looking for a partner, and I'm all right with being single."

Chapter

3

The next day I walked leisurely to Raffles Hotel. I arrived there before 9:00 a.m., and a lady staff guided me to a medium-size meeting room on the ground floor which resembled an office. It had a desk with a laptop on it. It also had a sofa and chairs. I took a seat on the sofa. After a few minutes, the King sauntered into the room.

"Good morning, Marianne."

"Good morning, Mr. King." I attempted to stand up out of respect for royalty, and he motioned for me to remain seated.

"Mr. King?" He chuckled. "I like that." He chose the seat next to the sofa. He was dressed casually in a loose white cotton shirt, certainly not in kingly fashion, but he still looked attractive. Anybody who would see him would regard him simply as a visiting tourist, and not a royal.

"Sorry about that. I've never really been in touch with royalty in my whole life," I explained.

"That's okay. I'm fine with it. Nobody has ever called me that," he replied, smiling. "How are you this morning?" He certainly had a nice smile, which any woman might find alluring.

"Great and raring to work. Your life must be very interesting."

"Well, it has its ups and downs, and never short of challenges. I printed out the first few chapters of the book for you to edit through. You can work on the desk with the laptop if you want."

"All right. First I want to know if we'll follow British or American English because it will definitely affect the spelling and expressions in the book."

"We'll use British English. It's our language in Marvella, also Italian. We're actually bilingual. I also speak French, Portuguese, and Spanish."

"Wow, the Romance Languages. You're multi-lingual then. I speak a little Spanish because my grandfather was Spanish. I notice that royals don't carry their family names. It's just Queen Elizabeth II or Edward VIII."

"That's right. I'm referred to as Franco V. Our family name is Morandi, but rarely used actually. This book I'm writing dates back to the era of my great great grandfather, who was Franco I."

"That makes it even more interesting."

"I appreciate your enthusiasm, Marianne. My ancestors led wholesome lives, so there may be just a few scandals, or none at all, chronicled in the book, unlike in other monarchies," he stated with a grin. "It's really meant for the appreciation of the people of Marvella of their history, and not for public consumption." I smiled at his reference to royal scandals.

"Did you go to Eton too like most royals?" I just had to ask.

"As a matter of fact, I did, and so did my son. I went on to Oxford for my Bachelor's degree, then to INSEAD in France for further studies and exposure to business. How about you? Where did you study?"

"I'm from the south of the Philippines, and I came to Metro Manila to study in the best schools in the country. I had a Catholic education."

"You seem highly educated. Did you work right away after graduation?"

"Well, after earning my Master's degree, I worked for a long time with a leading corporation. May I ask when you were crowned King of Marvella?"

"I became king at age 28 when my father passed away at the age of 62. Those details will be covered in the book."

"Such a young age to rule a monarchy. Am I asking too many questions, Mr. King?"

"Not at all. You deserve to know everything about me and my Kingdom as my book Editor."

"The people of Marvella must love you. You seem to be a good monarch. Matteo confirms that."

"Thank you for saying so, Marianne."

Just then a service staff entered the room to serve us coffee and pastries.

"You may want to have coffee and a bite while working. Feel free," he offered.

"Thank you. I'll take coffee. I'm a coffee drinker, but only until noon, otherwise I can't sleep at night."

"The same with me. By the way, before we start, we need to discuss your fee for this job."

"I don't really care how much I'm paid, so it's up to you. Just don't pay me too much because I don't need the money. One more question. Do you usually travel alone?"

"No, I'm not alone. There are always two bodyguards with me whom you probably didn't notice because they're almost invisible. They're just outside this room. Step out and check."

I went to the door, opened it, and peeked. Two foreign-looking men seated outside gave me furtive glances, and I concluded that they were the bodyguards.

"Did you spot them? I'd rather be alone, but my son insists that I take the bodyguards with me wherever I go, so they travel with me all the time. At the Rosetti condo, they stayed in the kitchen, so you didn't see them."

"They are easy to spot because they don't look Filipino, but perhaps not in other countries."

I opted to go through his manuscript on the sofa where I was comfortably seated, while he typed on the laptop. I was amazed with his writing capability. He had a way with words, and the data and events were well-researched. I made only minor editing and alterations on the early pages. Editing was a breeze.

"You write well, Mr. King," I complimented him.

"Thank you. That's a compliment coming from an Editor like you. Numbers are more of my expertise. It's almost lunchtime. Will you have lunch with me here?"

"I don't think lunch is part of our arrangement. Why don't I come back around 2:00 p.m. to give you time for rest?"

"All right, if that's what you want. See you here at 2:00 then."

As I left the room, the two bodyguards looked at me and stood, heading towards the room. I walked back to my condo and had a light lunch of leftovers from last night's dinner, which Sofia packed for me to take home so I didn't have to cook, she said. How thoughtful of her. I switched on the TV. Khaleesi snuggled next to me, and I dozed off for a new minutes. I woke up feeling revitalized. I freshened up and walked to Raffles. Mr. King was already in the room.

"Were you able to get some rest, Mr. King?", I asked him as I entered the room.

"Yes. Thanks for your concern. The *siesta* is a practice in my country. Everybody takes a nap after lunch. It's touted to make you live longer."

"It used to be a common practice here too. My late father always took his *siesta*."

"Well, did you have your *siesta*?"

"Just a cat nap with Khaleesi next to me."

"I'd like to see Khaleesi again before I go home."

"We can arrange that. I'm sure she wants to see you too. She seems to like you."

We resumed our work with him on the laptop and I going through what he had written. We made a lot of progress. His writing was easy to edit. We would not be able to finish the write-and-edit tasks during his limited stay, so we would resume through e-mail and possibly discuss matters on Face Time. When we are done with all these, he will concur with the printer in his Kingdom and provide the photos for the layout. He was very enthusiastic about this project, and his enthusiasm rubbed on me. After absorbing the facts in the book, I felt I was part of that Kingdom.

"Have you picked the title for your book?", I asked him.

"Not yet. Do you have any suggestions?"

"How about 'Marvella: A miracle to marvel at', which is its actual meaning?"

"That's a great idea, Marianne. I'll certainly consider it."

"I'd love to have an autographed copy of it. I feel I've become part of your book."

"You are definitely part of this book," he declared emphatically. "You'll get your copy, of course."

* * *

I was met by the incessant ringing of my phone as I stepped into my condo. It was Sofia. She wanted to know how my day went with the King.

"It went well", I reported. "He seems like a regular guy, and he doesn't make you feel that he's King, so I'm comfortable talking to him. I must have asked him a lot of questions, but he was very accommodating."

"I'm happy for you, Marianne. Do you think he's the guy you've been waiting for?"

"What are you saying, Sofia? I haven't been waiting for anybody. I do like being single."

"I know, but how do you feel about your connection with this guy? Any sparks?"

"Nothing monumental, but there's this feeling of ease. Well, you can't discount the fact that he's very good-looking, and he oozes with sex appeal. I can't understand why he hasn't remarried."

"Maybe he's looking for the right queen. It may just be you. Marianne."

"Oh, come on, Sofia. My thoughts haven't gone there. It's just nice looking at his handsome face and seeing his expression. I like those deep-blue eyes, and he does have a great smile too."

"That's a start, Marianne. I hope it goes further than that."

"He'll be here for only one more day. What can possibly happen?"

"Who knows? I just want to finally see my BFF with the right man."

"I'm not queen material, Sofia. Can you actually picture me sitting on a throne and living in a castle?"

"Why not? You're as pretty as any other queen."

"Marvella will not settle for an aging queen."

"That's the king's decision, not theirs. You don't look 60, Marianne. You don't even look 50. You've maintained your youthful looks, and you still make heads turn. You were the prettiest in our class. I've always admired you for not being aware of your beauty. You didn't even want to be a cover girl or a muse of a team. The King must be beguiled by your beauty."

"Thanks for boosting my ego, my friend. I guess I'm destined to stay single, and I'm happy with it right now. There's really nothing wrong with being single, is there? I'm perfectly comfortable with my chosen state. I don't have to answer to anybody."

Chapter

4

It was still early when I reached Raffles the next day, but the King was already there sipping his coffee. We greeted each other a pleasant good morning. He looked fresh as usual in a pin-striped shirt with denim jeans and loafers. I never imagined a king wearing denims. He was so down-to-earth, and he did look good in them. He did not strike me as vain, but he evidently had an excellent sartorial flair.

"Mr. King, have you been to the Philippines before?"

"Yes. This is my second time here, Marianne. Three years ago I was here on business, a trade transaction."

"Also *incognito*?"

"That's right," he answered with his engaging smile. "I often take a low profile." Then suddenly he produced a bag of Tootsie Pops and offered it to me. I could not believe it. He is a lollipop lover just like me.

"Do you know that I often have a lollipop in my handbag? When I watch a movie, I enjoy a lollipop as the lights go out. You do remind me of Telly Savalas in 'Kojak', but with hair of course."

He was amused with my statement and gave a hearty laugh. I liked his laugh. "I remember him. I enjoy a lollipop usually in private. A grandparent like me may strike a funny sight licking a lollipop in public." We both laughed at the image.

"And King at that," I added. It was such a private moment with the two of us licking lollipops.

"I meant to ask you if you need to do some shopping to bring home items from here. I can help you with that."

"That's kind of you, Marianne. Can you accompany me? You work so fast that we're practically finished with our work here with just a few pages left. We'll be done by this morning."

We resumed working for the entire morning, and I was done with editing the last page he finished writing just before noon. "Thanks for all your help, Marianne."

"You're welcome, Mr. King, but I'm not done with editing yet. I still have to go through the final copy before it goes to the printer."

"We can deal with that through e-mail much later." He rose from the desk and looked at me seriously, coming closer. "You've refused my invitation for lunch so far. I'm inviting you to dinner tonight, and you can't refuse me this time. It's my last day here." He was suddenly in a serious mood. I could sense it in his altered expression.

I paused for a few seconds. I was thinking that I should just accept his invitation since it was really his last day here. "Okay, I accept your invitation. I'll be back at 2:00 p.m., and after you've rested, I can take you shopping. Are you interested in buying pearls for people back home? They're of good quality here and not expensive."

"Pearls? That's a good idea. I have no wife or girlfriend, but I'm sure my daughter and nieces will like them."

I distinctly heard him say that he was unattached. Should I feel glad? Hold your horses, Marianne, I cautioned myself.

* * *

"Are you okay with walking some distance? The pearls are at the end of these buildings," I told the King.

"I've no problem with that. You know, I walk every afternoon in the area for exercise with my bodyguards in tow." We started walking towards Glorietta. One bodyguard walked ahead of us, and the other one behind us. They were dressed casually, so they were not as conspicuous, unlike the secret service agents in suits we see in movies and on TV. I guided the King towards Kultura in SM. I happened to know Janet, the supervisor in the pearls section, because I had purchased some items from them.

I told Janet, "*Pakitulungan siyang pumuli ng magandang perlas.*"

I turned to the King and said, "I told her to help you choose the lovely pearls. I'll be back here. I'll just pick a gift for Sofia's daughter Noelle."

Noelle is my godchild, and I got her a nice purse. When I returned to the pearls section, the items the King chose were laid out on the counter. There were a long strand of pearls, a double-strand one, a regular strand, two small bracelets, and three pairs of cuff links. These were of medium-size South Sea pearls. There were also a strand of fresh water pearls and seven pairs of cuff links.

"They're lovely," I commented.

"These ones are South Sea pearls, ma'am, for his family," Janet pointed at the evidently more expensive ones. "The fresh water ones are for his staff he said, but also of fine quality." I thanked Janet for helping the King with his choices. She placed each item in individual boxes, then accompanied the King to the cashier.

"Are you happy with your purchases?," I asked the King afterwards.

"Oh, yes. I got everything I needed to buy. I have gifts for my daughter, my son, my granddaughters, my grandson, my daughter-in-law, my son-in-law, my assistant, my valet, my butler, my housekeeper, my chef, my driver, and my body guards," he enumerates. "That's about it. All from one store. How convenient," he stated with satisfaction.

"That's a lot of people, and you even included the ones working with you."

"I don't really have too many staff compared with other monarchies. Hey, let's have coffee somewhere, shall we?"

"There's a Starbucks outlet on the way to your hotel." We both had decaf caramel *macchiato* and cookies there. He insisted on paying, and I gave him my senior card for a discount. The bodyguards were inconspicuously at a different table. I became aware that the ladies inside Starbucks were ogling him, and even the younger ones we encountered along the way gave him a second look, and he was not even conscious of it. His overall physique attracted attention since he was obviously a somebody and good-looking with his height and bearing.

"Do you have anywhere to go to from here?," he asked.

"I'll just walk home and take Khaleesi to the park. I owe her that."

"I'll meet you there, so I can see Khaleesi."

"By the way, are you a 'Game of Thrones' fan? You seem familiar with the name Khaleesi." I was curious to know.

"Absolutely. I've read all the books. I may sound juvenile, but I like adventure stories. I read a lot, and I've read 'The Hunger Games' and Rick Riordan's books. I also read thought-provoking books, some related to biographies and also about business."

"And I thought I'm the only one acting juvenile. I followed on Netflix the series on royals, like 'The Crown'. I enjoyed 'Downton Abbey', not exactly royal, but aristocratic. I'm also an avid follower of 'Outlander'."

His eyes widened. "Marianne, you're a revelation. I happen to watch all those. I always anticipate their new seasons." He looked at me with genuine appreciation and I felt suffused with an indescribable feeling of belonging to his league.

For a moment, I could sense that he liked me. How is it possible that this man had the same interests as mine? If I liked him earlier, I liked him even more now. There was just one major problem. He is King, and I am just an ordinary commoner.

* * *

We parted ways at Landmark, and I proceeded to my condo. I needed to talk to Sofia. I related to her the events that transpired today.

"I just can't believe that we like the same things, read the same books, and watch the same series," I confessed.

"That's a really good sign, Marianne. Even liking lollipop? Wow, what other signs do you want?"

"Sofia, you know that nothing can come out of this. I can't have any serious connection with a King."

"What's wrong with that? You always said that you need to fall in love first. Well, King or not, do you have feelings for him?"

"I don't know because I've never fallen in love before. Why are we discussing this? I don't even know how he feels towards me."

"He obviously likes you, Marianne. Are you going to see him still?"

"Yes, later this afternoon when I'll walk Khaleesi to the park. I'll meet him there because he wants to see Khaleesi."

"See that? He's even interested in your dog." This made me laugh.

"Then I'll have dinner with him tonight since he'll be leaving tomorrow."

"At the dinner tonight, I believe you'll know how you feel towards him. I can sense that. Keep cool, and call me tonight after your dinner no matter how late."

* * *

Khaleesi and I arrived at the park before 5:00 p.m. She suddenly became attentive and pulled me along. Sure enough, the King was seated on the bench, and Khaleesi was all excited to see him as if he was a long-lost friend. I had never seen her this excited before with anyone. I sat next to him while he played with Khaleesi and patted her, to her delight. This time I noticed the bodyguards in a nearby bench.

"Why does she seem to know you so well?" I questioned. "She has always been an introvert dog. Maybe she knows you're royalty?"

"Haha. You can be funny, Marianne. I like your sense of humor."

"Do you have dogs, Mr. King?"

"Yes, we have a kennel of dogs. They have their own area to run around, but not inside the castle. I visit them often because I love dogs."

"Maybe Khaleesi could sense in you that you're an ally."

"Remember you're having dinner with me tonight," he reminded me before we parted. "I'll meet you at the lobby at 7:00 p.m."

"Sure. I'll see you there."

* * *

I took a shower first, then I donned on a simple sleeveless black shift dress of knee-length. I wore it with a dressy black shawl. I was at the lobby 10 minutes early, and the King was already there standing tall, wearing an open-necked white long-sleeved shirt with a navy blue jacket over it, and smiling at me. He certainly looked dashing. Gazing at him made my heart skip a beat.

"You look stunning," he commented as he looked me over, and I felt a blush coming on.

After greeting each other, we did not talk much anymore as we walked towards the elevator which brought us to the 9th floor at the Mereio Restaurant.

"Have you been here before?" he inquired.

"No, this is my first time here. I've been only to the buffet restaurant downstairs. This has an elegant ambience."

The waiter guided us to a table for two. It is a Provencal-inspired, brasserie-style restaurant offering French cuisine with Mediterranean influence.

"Do you have any food preferences? No allergies?" He wanted to know.

"None whatsoever."

"Good, so you can order whatever you want." The waiter took our orders. Then the King produced a rectangular box and handed it to me.

"What's this?" I reacted with increasing curiosity.

"It's my gift for you for being an excellent Editor."

"You don't have to do this, Mr. King. All I did was minor editing."

"I want to. Open it." I opened the box and inside it was the double-strand pearl necklace he purchased earlier. "Let me put it on you." He then went to my side, and I lifted my below-the-shoulder hair so he could clasp the necklace on my neck. I was conscious of his fingers touching my neck as if a current briefly passed through me.

"Thank you. Are you always this gallant? I don't deserve this."

"Of course, you do, but you may already have a pearl necklace."

"Yes, but not a double-strand one as exquisite as this."

"It looks lovely on you." Then he handed me an envelope. "One more thing, this is the half payment for your service. You will get the other half after the completion of the book. I understand that's how it's done." I thanked him and put the envelope in my purse without opening it.

I was already feeling jittery before dinner. So much had happened. We had hot soup for starters, then green salad. I ordered the smoked salmon to avoid dealing with not-easy-to-eat foods, like prawns or lobster. He had the pan-seared duck. We both had apple tart with vanilla ice cream for dessert. I am not a big eater, so the meal was more than satisfactory.

"Marianne, may I ask you some questions?" he began during dinner.

"What kind of questions?"

"Mainly about you. I just want to know more about you. That is, if you don't mind."

"Not at all. I've nothing to hide."

"Did you have past relationships?"

"You mean, did I have boyfriends? Well, in my younger days, I had a couple of boyfriends, but nothing serious. I was quite young then."

"You never married. Why, may I ask?"

"It's a personal choice. Sofia knows me quite well, and she is fully aware that I'd marry only for love. The thing is, I've not fallen in love with anybody, but I really have no problem with staying single."

"You're such a beautiful person, and you must have had a lot of suitors."

"You're making me blush. Yes, I had suitors, but no sparks. I'll never marry for convenience. What can possibly come out of a marriage without love?"

"You're amazing, and you're so different. I've never met anyone like you. I like you a lot, Marianne." He looked at me with a soulful expression, and my heart just melted.

"Thanks for the like. I like you too. You don't make me feel uncomfortable with your stature," I openly admitted.

"I'm just a normal human being like everyone else, except for this title. Don't allow it to intimidate you," he uttered with a smile.

Our dinner and interesting conversation lasted for two hours. We rode the elevator to the lobby to say our goodbyes. I was feeling somewhat sad that I may not see him again. He asked for my calling card with my home address, e-mail address, and mobile phone number on it. He promised to communicate with me on Face Time. Royals shun social media as much as possible, so they do not use Facebook.

"Well, this is it. Goodbye, Marianne. May I give you a hug?" he sought my permission with hope written on his face.

Without hesitation, I advanced into his arms. It was a 30-second tight hug, and I breathed in his manly cologne and his pleasant natural scent. It was wonderful. Before he released me, he planted a firm kiss on my cheek. It was a shy moment on my part, and I just looked up at him shyly and smiled.

"Are you going to be all right walking alone at night? I can walk you home," he offered.

"No, it's not necessary. Makati is a safe place and the stores are still open. Thank you, but I'll be okay."

I was giddy walking to my condo. I opened the envelope from him as I got home. In it was a manager's check for P50,000. So, he intended to pay me P100,000 for the entire job? It was far too much.

* * *

"How did it go?" Sofia anxiously inquired on the phone.

"Very well, and I'm more confused than ever." I repeated to her the accounts of tonight's dinner.

"He said he likes you a lot? That's practically a declaration of his feelings for you. How do you feel towards him?"

"I don't know, Sofia. I've never felt like this before."

"You may already be in love, BFF," Sofia stated teasingly. "At long last."

"I don't even know how being in love feels."

"You'll know eventually."

Chapter

5

I hardly slept a wink. The King dominated my thoughts. I kept asking myself, "Am I in love?" When I uttered this aloud, Khaleesi looked at me questioningly. I asked her, "Am I in love with the King, Khaleesi?", and she whimpered positively as if she understood my feelings. I overslept and I was roused from sleep by my ringing phone at past 10:00 a.m. It was Sofia.

"Good morning, Sofia. I couldn't sleep last night, so I overslept," I yawned.

"Are you fully awake now?"

"Sort of. Why?"

"I have good news for you." She was practically singing her sentence. "The King and Matteo saw each other at breakfast this morning before he boarded his royal jet. Matteo said that the King talked most of the time about you. He admitted that he's smitten by you." That awakened me and made me sit up.

"You must be kidding."

"No, I'm not. I'm just repeating to you what he told Matteo. Great news. Are you happy?"

"I am, but I'm still confused. I need time to analyze all this. We'll still be communicating online because my editing is not yet done, and I'm now feeling more anxious than ever. I'm not ready for this, Sofia."

"Take it slowly, Marianne. Just be yourself. He likes you for who you are."

* * *

My day was taken up by activities I neglected to attend to when my time was occupied with editing for the past two days. I had lector duties at my parish. It was a weekend, and this was when I volunteered for charity work for a local nongovernment organization (NGO). When the day was over, I was exhausted and just plopped myself on the sofa, and Khaleesi joined me.

I dozed off for about an hour. I dreamt of the King. He haunted me even in my dreams. In my dream, he was extending his hand towards me, and when I was about to touch him, he disappeared into thin air. I searched everywhere, but failed to find him. I woke up with sadness. I do not believe in dreams because mine are usually silly and hard-to-believe scenarios. I called Sofia.

"I dreamt of the King during my nap this afternoon, and it wasn't a positive dream," I shared with her. "Do you suppose it means something somber?" I relived my dream to her.

"I thought you don't believe in dreams, Marianne."

"I really don't, but this one was so vivid. It was like telling me that I can't reach him. I couldn't even touch him. It was utterly eerie."

"Banish it from your mind, and just look at the positive side. Dreams won't determine your future."

"Okay, okay. I'll think positive."

"Matteo has a business dinner tonight, and they're all men, so I'm not joining him. Let's have dinner at Dulcinea, my treat, and we can have our favorite *paella*."

"Fine. See you there at 7:00 p.m.?"

At dinner, I asked Sofia to familiarize me with the signs of love. "How do you know you're really in love with someone?"

"The signs are usually obvious. Is he in your thoughts most of the time? Has this particular person become very important to you? Do you have similar interests? Do you espouse the same values? Does he make you smile and laugh? When he enters the room, is your attention riveted to him? There are myriad ways, Marianne."

"I can't include pursuing the same dreams in your list of signs because I'm not chasing dreams anymore at this age. Does a king have dreams, I wonder?"

"Who knows? Maybe his dream now is to find his Queen."

"However, I can answer 'yes' to all that you mentioned, Sofia. I can distinguish it from infatuation or crush, again because I'm old enough to know the difference."

"You'll certainly know if the feeling is genuine. It's a wait-and-see situation. We'll wait for his move."

"Okay. Somehow you calmed me down. Still I wouldn't know what to do if he does pursue me."

"One step at a time, Marianne. Ask yourself what's the most important thing to you. I experienced that dilemma when Matteo proposed to me. I chose to relocate and be with him. I never regretted my decision because I love him, and he became the most important person in my life. Your situation is far more complex than mine because it involves royalty. It will be an entirely new life for you if you marry into royalty. It's going to be like some sort of a social makeover."

"Sofia, we're already discussing marriage when he hasn't even expressed his feelings for me."

"I can predict it will lead to that. I sensed this when he revealed to Matteo how much he likes you. I don't believe he'll take his sweet time because he's not getting any younger. Anyway, let's wait and see."

* * *

Two days went by and I still had zero communication with the King. Thankfully, my anxiety was somewhat diffused when I got drawn into a whirl of social functions with former classmates and officemates. My personal thoughts were drowned out by the chattering about recent trips made by my friends and the continuing rife discussions on political events and characters.

Then by late afternoon, I received a message from the King on Viber. He wrote, "How are you, Marianne? I'm missing you. I can't wait to communicate with you. I got caught up in a series of Town Hall meetings to discuss pressing concerns in the Kingdom. I plan to get in touch with you on Face Time. Our time difference is about seven hours. So, if I call you at 11:00 a.m., that will be 6:00 p.m. there. Are you all right with that?"

I responded promptly, "That's perfectly fine. I'll wait for your call. I hope you're well."

"Thanks, Marianne. I'm busy, but well and fine. I can't wait to see you and talk to you on Face Time," he replied.

His admission that he missed me and that he was eager to see and hear me were enough to warm my heart. While waiting for our Face Time hook-up, I retouched my make-up and freshened up a bit to look presentable to the King of Marvella.

"Hello, Marianne. You're lovely as ever. I do miss you terribly. Did you miss me?" he asked as we got connected on Face Time. He appeared distinguished-looking in a more formal outfit than his usual attire here. He must have come from an event in the Kingdom. My heart did a somersault at his handsome sight. I have always been a goner for tall and handsome men, and he fits the bill.

"I miss you too, Mr. King."

"Before anything else, can you start calling me Franco?"

"Isn't that being too familiar? What will people say? Remember, you're King."

"I don't care what people will say. That's what I want you to call me. From now on I'm Franco to you. Besides, I want you to be on a familiar level with me."

"Okay, if that's what you prefer."

"That's what I want. My dear Marianne, that shouldn't be too difficult considering how I feel towards you."

"How you feel towards me?" I threw back his statement at him. "I don't seem to have any idea about that."

"I can't mask my feelings for you anymore. I'm strongly attracted to you, and I'm ready to profess my feelings for you." I was taken aback by his declaration, and I was rendered speechless. Some seconds passed.

"Say something, my dear. If you're not attracted to me, that's all right with me."

"No, that's not it because I find you very attractive." He gave me a pleased expression. "I just can't understand why you like me because I'm 60 years old. Men usually chase young women."

"I'm not like other men. I admire and appreciate you for who and what you are. You're beautiful, smart, and funny too. You are a decent woman, Marianne, and you have a very pleasing personality. You don't even look 60, but I don't really care. I confess I've never met anyone like you. My dear, lovely Marianne, you literally captured my heart. I confess I've fallen in love with you, and I'm now officially courting you." For a moment, I was again speechless. I did not know if I could handle this.

"What can I say? Give me a little time to allow everything to sink in."

"Take all the time you need, but frankly I don't want to wait too long. I'll try to contact you every day at this time, so goodbye for now, Marianne. Remember, I love you." Our conversation lasted for about an hour. He asked me what I had been busy with and he was sincerely interested in my activities. It ended at just the right time for his lunch and for my dinner. I was left in a state of confusion after our conversation. No man ever had this effect on me.

Chapter

6

I could not move nor eat after my conversation with the King or Franco. I was filled with an overwhelming feeling of joy. I fully realized at that very moment that I was also in love, and with this man. In totality, he is easy to fall in love with. It took me a few minutes to call Sofia, and I shared with her my conversation with the King. She was more excited than I was.

"Alleluia! That's it, Marianne. The next stage will be the proposal."

"Things are going so fast. I don't know if I'm prepared for this."

"You've been ready for more than 30 years, and now that you've met the right man, you can no longer say no to this. Follow your heart, Marianne."

* * *

During the day, I received a package by DHL from King Franco. He sent me a box of Swiss chocolates with a note saying "I can't send you ice cream, so I'm sending you the next best thing. I hope you like chocolates. Love, Franco." His message brought a smile to my face. I like being pampered and wooed, especially by someone I do love. I happen to like chocolates too.

I finally knew what Sofia meant about being in love. I could not wait for 6:00 p.m. every day to see him and talk to him on Face Time. I practically ached for his presence, and I had to be content with communicating with him online.

I was the first to speak when King Franco came online. "Thanks for the chocolates. I love chocolates too. How did you know?"

"Just a hunch. We seem to like the same things, so I figured that includes chocolates too. We're obviously compatible."

"I meant to tell you that the check you gave me is way too much. Please don't give me anymore check. This is more than enough."

"Are you sure? It was just the monetary measure of your work. Okay, now let's change the subject. Tell me frankly how you feel towards me."

"Now?"

"Yes, now, Marianne." I became fidgety and self-conscious.

"I told you how I feel about you yesterday. You must know that your family name 'Diez' means '10' in Spanish. You're a '10' to me, Marianne." I become even more self-conscious and covered my face with my hands to hide my blush.

"I haven't blushed like this since I was a teenager," I confessed to him, and he laughed out loud.

"Does this reaction mean you love me too?"

"Oh, Franco, I'm so confused now. I've never been in love before and this feeling is so intense and overwhelming."

"I'm glad to hear that. It's time for us to have a relationship. We're not getting any younger. Will you be my girlfriend, Marianne?"

"This is indeed whirlwind, and I can't help but be scared."

"Don't be. I promise I'll never hurt you. I'm sincere about my feelings for you, and I truly love you. I ask you again, Marianne, will you be my girlfriend?"

"Give me a minute." I paused for a few seconds, then I made a deep sigh and replied, "Yes,' nodding my head. He grinned from ear to ear.

"I wish you were here with me so I can hug and kiss you. One more thing, may I hear you say that you love me? It's of great importance to me to hear it from you."

"I do love you, Franco." He rewarded me with the biggest smile. I have a King for a boyfriend, and a very handsome one at that. It is something I can never brag or even hint about for fear of media repercussion.

* * *

My best friend and confidante Sofia was the happiest person when she found out how I sealed my relationship with King Franco.

"We have to be careful that this does not leak out to the media," I cautioned her. "If they learn he's a King, they'll have a field day. I'm glad he always travels *incognito*. You and Matteo are the only ones who know. I can't even tell my own brother yet. I hate publicity myself."

"Don't worry, I'll warn Matteo about it. He'll always protect his King."

"Look what's happening to England's royalty. They're hounded by *paparazzi* and all sorts of stories are written about them, often criticizing their every move. I can't live with that. I'm glad King Franco's Kingdom is small and perhaps overlooked, but a news-worthy item can stir things up."

"I'm behind you on this, Marianne. We'll keep it very private, and nobody will know until you've wed the King and have moved to Marvella."

"Sofia, I haven't looked that far. I haven't even considered living in Marvella. Of course, I'd want to be by Franco's side wherever he is."

"Oh my goodness, Marianne, you truly are in love. I'm very happy for you."

"I know that if I do marry him, it will be a major move for me. I will be transported to a different world. That will mean an entirely new life, but I can't imagine now life without him."

"Take it as an exciting adventure beside the person you love. How romantic can it be?"

"He's the only one that matters, and he's my top priority now."

* * *

On my third Face Time encounter with King Franco, he was more amorous, and my feelings for him grew even stronger.

"My darling Marianne, what exactly made you love me? I just want to know what qualities I have which captured an elusive heart like yours."

"Franco, can't you see how good a person you are?, and you're even King. You're never condescending, you're sincere, and kind. You don't behave like a monarch at all. Add to that your good looks, of course, and the fact that we have the same interests. You're easy to love. You're not a difficult person to talk to and get along with. Even Khaleesi likes you." He laughed at this.

"What else?" He was probing.

"You're also controlling."

"I'm controlling?", he questioned me with raised eyebrows. "I don't understand. What do you mean by that?" He gave me a surprised look, like he did not anticipate a statement like this from me.

"Don't get me wrong. I like controlling. I like a man who tells me what to do. I find that a strength in a man. You're King, so being controlling is not a bad thing really."

"My darling, I'm learning a lot from you. You never cease to amaze me."

"I've always been independent and headstrong, and my mom used to tell me that. Now at my age, I like a man who will lead me and whom I can look up to. I want to look up to you, Franco. You're King of my heart."

"I want to kiss you right now. Wait till we see each other again. I plan to make a trip there in the coming week after settling the urgent issues in the Kingdom."

I got excited when he said he planned to make a trip here next week. That is quite soon. His threat of kissing me excited me even more. I anticipated his kisses. I had heard and read about soul mates before, and I did not think much about it. Now I am certain more than ever that soul mates do exist. I am 100% sure that Franco is my soul mate, and a higher being brought us together and let our paths cross.

Chapter

7

We had no regular Face Time sessions in the next days, but he sent me a message on Viber that his time was taken up by a series of meetings, and to expect him soon. I responded that he should give priority to his duties before anything else, and he thanked me for my advice.

As I stepped into my condo building mid-afternoon after coming from the supermarket, the Concierge informed me that there was a delivery of roses for me. The staff accompanied me to my condo with it. I read the attached card. It was from Franco with the message, "Missing you a lot. Love, Franco." They were lovely large pink roses with an orangey tint. I wondered how he sent them. Then my cellphone rang.

"Hello, Marianne. Do you like the roses?"

"Franco, where are you?", I inquired anxiously.

"I'm in your building downstairs. May I see you?"

"Oh, my goodness. What a surprise. May I talk to the Concierge?" I requested the Concierge to allow my visitor to go up to my unit because we had strict security. Franco's bodyguards waited at the lobby.

As I opened my door, Franco immediately enfolded me into his arms and kissed me wildly. He could not stop kissing me, and I responded with equal ardor. We continued to kiss, and I enjoyed it immensely. I had never been kissed like this before in my life. He was a very good kisser. He could be tender, then intense the next minute. Khaleesi was jumping up and down, maybe wondering what was happening. After some time, I pushed Franco away gently and led him to the sofa. Khaleesi was beside herself upon seeing him. He sat down, turned his attention to her, and patted her.

"Wow, is that how it's like to be kissed by a King?," I blurted out, and he laughed heartily as I rested my head on his shoulder and wrapped my arm around his waist.

"There's more where it comes from," he answered with a twinkle in his eyes. "Do you like kissing me?"

"I didn't know it can be this wonderful." Then he pulled me closer to him and kissed me again with unbridled passion, which shot my emotions sky-high. "I love you, darling," he kept saying. We continued kissing until we were breathless.

"Your kisses are worth the trip. I can't be in the country long because I still have unfinished business in the Kingdom. You're having dinner with me tonight at Raffles. Is that okay with you? Do you want me to pick you up?"

"That's okay. I can walk."

"I'll meet you at the hotel lobby." He rose and surveyed my place. "Hey, you have a nice place here. I was busy kissing you that I didn't notice it." He shifted into a teasing mood.

"Thanks. I decorated it myself." He kissed me firmly again before he left my condo.

* * *

I was shaken by all that kissing. I called Sofia to update her on the unexpected incident.

"He's here? Don't you see, he may be here only to propose to you, Marianne. He seems to be in a rush. A great kisser, huh? Good for you."

"I'm still up in the clouds after all that kissing. It's wonderful."

"I can just imagine. Don't forget to call me tonight after your dinner. I'm anxious to know if he'll propose as I predict."

* * *

Franco gave me a discreet and brief kiss on the lips at the hotel lobby. He had on a black jacket over a beige shirt. I wore a floral pink dress with a matching short plain blazer. We held hands walking towards the elevator to Mireio. That meant that we were truly sweethearts now because a man and a woman do not hold hands in the Philippines unless they are sweethearts. He asked me earlier to pick the restaurant, and I told him I was okay with going to the same restaurant because we haven't really tried all their dishes, and he added that he also wanted to go back to this place because there was something he liked to show me there. That aroused my curiosity.

"This is an interesting restaurant," I commented. "I googled it and discovered that it's named after a famous poem about a failed forbidden love between Mereio, a rich farmer's daughter, and Vincent, a simple basket weaver."

"Is that right? That's an intriguing love story."

For our entrees, Franco ordered the roasted blue marlin and I had the *primavera risotto*. After dinner and conversation, he led me up to the 10th floor terrace. The view was awesome and the city lights glimmered in the night. This was what he meant earlier about showing me something. He hugged me from behind and it was good. We admired the glittery view for a moment. Then he slowly turned me around and went down on one knee, which caught me by surprise even if I could sense that he was somehow up to something.

"My darling Marianne, will you marry me?" I was uncomfortable about the kneeling.

"Franco, I'll give you my answer if you'll get up please." He stood up immediately.

"Okay. Will you say yes to becoming my Queen? I love you with all my heart. I adore you. *Non posso vivere senza de ti.* I can't live without you."

"I'm touched. Yes, I'll marry you. I love you too very much." He wrapped me into a tight embrace and gave me a long kiss. He slipped into my finger the engagement ring which he said belonged to his late mother with a good-size diamond stone on it. I knew by its sheer size it was priceless, but I am not the kind of person who measures or puts value on things. I was simply deliriously happy that he gave me an engagement ring and asked me to be his wife.

"You know, I came back only to propose to you. I told my children about my plans, and they readily approved. They trust my choice. I want you to be my wife as soon as possible. Is one month enough time for you to prepare for our wedding?"

"I want that too. I do have some concern about the venue. I don't think it's a good idea for us to get married here because the local media might get wind of who you are and we'll lose our privacy. I don't want you involved in any publicity."

"Then we can get married in Marvella."

"We can do that, but is it possible to have a small wedding with just our family members and no fanfare? Is it required for a king to have a grand wedding?"

"Not necessarily. I can introduce you to everybody in the Kingdom after we're married. Don't women usually dream of a big wedding?" he questioned me.

"Not I. It's just that I don't want you to spend on a lavish wedding. A small one will require less preparation and I'll be happy with that. I just want to be married to you."

"My only wish is to make you my wife at the soonest possible time too, my darling."

"So we agree on that, and on just a simple ceremony with our families. On my side of the family, there will be only Matteo and Sofia plus my brother, who will walk me to the altar since we have no more living parents. No need for a large entourage or even an invitation because it may get into the wrong hands. I prefer a quiet wedding."

"Okay then. We can have the ceremony at the small chapel in the castle. We have plenty of rooms in the castle, so Matteo, Sofia and your brother can also stay there. I have to return home tomorrow. I'll communicate with you, and you can tell me the expenses needed."

"No need to worry about that. I'll take care of my wedding dress and plane fare."

"You're such an uncomplicated woman, and you have no demands. I love you so much. No, I don't want you to fly commercial. I'll send the royal jet to fly you and your party to Marvella."

"I don't really mind taking a commercial flight. I don't want to bother you any further."

"It's no bother at all. The royal jet is at the King's disposal."

"All right. You're already making me feel like royalty."

"You're going to be royalty when you marry me," he emphasized. So, I could not refuse his offer. That is what I mean by "controlling", and I appreciate it.

"Franco, one month is really a long time not to be together after we've found each other. I already feel sad about your leaving."

He hugged me tightly. "You know, missing you will be the hardest part for me. You pick the date you want and I'll make the arrangements there. No longer than one month. Okay, love?" He touched my chin and sought my lips. Oh, how I love this man.

He accompanied me to the lobby where we said our goodbyes. We kissed and had a long hug. Anyone around observing us would be inclined to conclude that it was a kind of goodbye, judging from the sad expression painted on our faces.

Chapter

8

"Sofia, it's set. We're getting married in a month's time in Marvella. I convinced Franco that we'll have more privacy there. Will you be my maid-of-honor? Actually, matron-of-honor."

"Of course, Marianne. I'm honored," she reacted excitedly.

"You, Matteo, and my brother will be my only guests. I told Franco I want a small simple wedding with just our families."

"I'm just as excited. You know that I've never been to Marvella, which is Matteo's birth place?"

"This is a good opportunity for you to visit Marvella."

"Of course. I can suggest to Matteo that we can go on a holiday to make most of our trip."

"Good idea. Do you know that Franco insisted on sending the royal jet to fly us to Marvella?"

"Wow, that's indeed some royal treatment."

"I know. Hey, Sofia, will you help me with my wedding dress? I may try to design it, but I need a *coutourier* to execute my design. Do you know of a reliable one? I don't need a celebrity *coutourier*."

"I'd love to help you with that. I'll contact my friend *coutourier* who may be able to take this on. I can't help getting all excited about your wedding."

"No word about it to our friends please."

"You can always count on me. Besides, we don't need to tell the *coutourier* whom you're marrying, just that you're getting married in another country."

"That's more like it. We only have a month to prepare, so I need to act fast."

* * *

The following day, I talked to my only brother Jesse, who is older than I. I told him that I was getting married in Europe in a month's time, but I did not divulge the details. I would tell him everything in time.

"Are you marrying a foreigner?" Jesse wanted to know.

"Yes. Don't ask me any more questions. I'll explain everything to you later, so I want you to trust me. I have my reasons. I do love this person very much."

"Okay, I trust you. You've always been quite secretive. I don't believe you'll make a harsh decision this late in life. I'd be glad to walk you to the altar."

"Thanks, Jess. I appreciate that, and for trusting me."

* * *

I put my time and attention on my forthcoming wedding. I decided to wear a wedding gown made of *jusi*, a Philippine material, to project my heritage. I described to the *coutourier* how I wanted it to look. I designed a fitting bodice with a slightly dropped waistline that flowed into a full skirt, featuring successive wavy folds. I expressed to him that I wanted dainty embroidery on the bodice and the abbreviated sleeves and repeated generously at the hemline of the skirt. I opted for an open neckline so I could wear the pearl necklace from Franco. I did not like the *bustier* style favored by most brides, and no *bling-bling* or a train for me. Sofia's friend *coutourier* was okay with my preferences, and he was happy to execute my design.

Sofia willingly accompanied me to the *coutourier's* shop and for my fitting. I needed only a single fitting, and it fitted me perfectly. Since *jusi* is of beige color, I looked for the right shoes to match it, and I got the wedge type that I favored for comfort. My gown was ready in less than three weeks, and I was happy with the result. I gushed in awe as I put it on, and so did Sofia. It was simply beautiful and exquisite. The dress accentuated my slim figure. I hoped Franco will love it too.

It was not easy packing my personal things and possessions since I could not bring all with me. I had to choose the clothes and shoes which I could wear in Marvella. I could come back for the rest at some future time. There were some arrangements to make. Renting out my condo entailed some attention, so I allowed my niece Mia, who worked in Makati, to occupy it. She is Jesse's daughter. I also offered the use of my Prius to Jesse's son Rafael, so that was a load off my mind.

I did not want to leave Khaleesi behind, and Franco said I could bring her with me because the castle has an open kennel for their dogs, and she will fit in well there. I could take her with me in a cage on the royal jet.

Then there were some presents to buy. I had a pair of special cufflinks made for Franco with his initials, which was my present for my groom, a *capiz* box for his daughter Tania, a desk pen set with *capiz* inlay for his son Franz, and small tokens for his grandkids and his children's spouses. A week before my scheduled trip, I was more than ready and eager to see Franco again.

* * *

With my tight pre-wedding schedule, I had to give up my other commitments in Church, the nongovernment organization for my charity work, and my regular lunches with former classmates. I told them that I was taking a job abroad and will be away for a good length of time, and I was not lying either. I promised to keep in touch with my friends when my feet are firmly planted on foreign soil. They did not question me any further and all wished me luck.

The only activities I did not give up were my painting and reading. I read before going to bed, and I painted during the day. I talked to Franco online, and he asked about my schedule.

"I'm continuing with my painting right now," I mentioned to him.

"You paint? I don't believe this. Do you know that I paint too? Darling, you're really full of surprises."

"Is that right? You surprise me too. I can bring only my paints and brushes there, but not my easel and canvas."

"Don't worry about that. I'll get you an easel and canvas. We can even paint together. I look forward to the painting sessions with my wife."

"That would be nice," I replied. Referring to me as his wife secretly touched me.

"What are the subjects of your paintings?"

"Landscapes, flowers, and still life. I'm not good with people and animals, but I want to learn. I love horses."

"We have horses in the royal stable, and I'm sure you'd want to see them. Do you ride?"

"My father used to have a horse on which I learned to ride when I was a child, but that was a very long time ago."

"We'll go riding in Marvella. There are so many things I'd want to do and enjoy here with you."

"Oh, Franco, I can't wait to be your wife and share your life. You know, we have so much to learn about each other still, about our respective families for instance. I have only one sibling, my older brother

Jesse. You already told me about your education, but not much about your family. Do you all live in the castle?"

"Yes, we do. It's big enough for all of us. What else do you want to know?"

"Just out of curiosity, do you dress up for dinner like in 'Downton Abbey'?"

"No, nothing like that. We don't actually follow some royal practices. We usually have dinner together, but we dress casually, except when we have a party in the castle."

"I want to be involved in your activities as much as I can. Where do I fit in?"

"I want that too, darling. I go riding, play tennis and golf. I fence and I play polo on occasions. I also go to the gym regularly and I walk daily in the castle grounds."

"I played a little tennis when I was younger, but I want to learn golf. Can I join you in your walking and in the gym?"

"I'd like that very much. I'll teach you how to play golf. I'm already eager to have you join me."

"You can also involve me in office work if you want. We still have to finish your book, remember?"

"Of course. It will be a pleasure working with you now on that," he answered with a smile. "However, we have to put the book on hold as we concentrate on our wedding."

"What is the weather like in Marvella? It was in June when I first went to Italy and it was starting to get hot."

"It's the same as Rome, but more breezy since it's an island kingdom. It's Mediterranean climate. Hot during summer towards July and cool in January."

I wanted to ask him about his late wife, but it might sound nosy at this early stage, so I decided to reserve that question after we were married. I knew that I still had many more questions to ask him. The fact was that we barely knew each other, so this wedding was a gamble for both of us, and we were just depending on our strong feelings for each other. On my part, I was actually following my heart as Sofia advised. I could only rely on Matteo's word that Franco is a "good man."

Franco is the only man who awakened my feelings of love towards the opposite sex which I did not know I would experience as intensely as this. I had not loved anybody this much before, and I was not even looking for a partner. This was truly a "leap of faith".

I was aware that moving to another country with a different culture entailed some degree of adjustment on my part, so just the thought of it could be frightening. Sofia convinced me that it is how you look at it. She stressed that if I take it as challenging, it could also turn out to be fulfilling. I am glad to have a friend like her who enlightens me.

PART 2

The Kingdom

Chapter

1

My small wedding party boarded the royal jet Franco sent for us. It was more or less a 12-hour flight, and we all enjoyed our conversation and food on board. We also got a shuteye the rest of the way. We decided to be in Marvella two days before the wedding. Jesse and I sat next to each other on the jet. As soon as we were airborne, I revealed to him whom I was marrying to satisfy his curiosity.

"So this is the secret you were keeping from me," he commented.

"I couldn't tell you then because I was guarding Franco's identity. Just imagine if Philippine media learns of it. I hope you understand," I explained to him. He smiled and assured me that he was happy for me.

Before landing, the pilot circled the plane over Marvella. We viewed the Kingdom from above, which is separated by a long bridge that connects it to Italy.

It gave me the impression of a fairy tale setting or something imaginary, like Shangri-La or Brigadoon we had read about, but this one is real.

My Franco was conspicuously all smiles at the tarmac as our plane touched down. He kissed and hugged me tightly. I was overwhelmed with joy upon seeing and touching him. I introduced my brother to him as we deplaned. Jesse still could not believe that I was marrying a real King.

We were driven to the castle in two vehicles with a security vehicle ahead of us and another one behind us. I observed that the castle's iron gates had "M" intricately carved on them. It could stand for "Morandi" or "Marvella." The head butler, Mr. Creely, welcomed us at the door and ushered us in. The Morandi family's coat-of-arms displayed in the foyer instantly caught my eye as we entered the castle. I did not expect the castle to be of such magnitude and of incredible dimensions. I was dumbfounded as we stepped in, and all I could say repeatedly was "Wow". It was well-maintained and tastefully decorated with high ceilings and wide spaces. A grand piano stood at one end of the main drawing room.

Franco introduced us to his family – his son Franz and daughter Tania, with their spouses, and his adorable grandkids. They were very welcoming and genuinely glad to meet us. His son Franz is a young version of him, without the beard, and just as good-looking. He will eventually become Franco VI when he becomes King, but they refer to him now as "Franz" so as not to confuse him with his father. His daughter Tania is a stunning beauty and as regal as a royal. His children inherited his striking features. I noticed that royals had a certain bearing characteristic of aristocracy. Perhaps even if nobody tells me that Franco is a King, I would be inclined to judge him as a person of prominence by the way he carries himself.

We arrived in Marvella before noontime, so we were served lunch at the dining area. Franco occupied the seat at the head of the long table, and he guided me to the seat to his right. There was animated conversation, especially after Franco's son and daughter discovered that Matteo is a native of Marvella, and he knew some of the families and people familiar to them. They even had common friends. Sofia was glad that Matteo was able to visit his birth place, and she could see the joy of being home registered on his face.

After lunch, Franco led us to the drawing room, where we had coffee. Then he updated us on our schedule, which his assistant Carlo organized for us. In the afternoon, we will go on a tour of Marvella and visit its tourist spots. It will resume the next day with shopping included. Franco disclosed that the people of Marvella did not know about his wedding plans. The palace staff were sworn to secrecy, so it would not leak out before his formal announcement on national TV after our return from our honeymoon. Everything was meticulously planned, and I did not have to do anything on my part. I was already being treated like a Queen, but it had not dawned on me yet how it felt to be one.

Only Carlo accompanied us on our tour. The King does not normally roam the Kingdom, except on certain important occasions. Still, I missed his company. We learned of Marvella's rich history, and we visited its massive museum. It was such a magnificent and picturesque Kingdom with a profusion of greenery and majestic landscapes. Carlo was quite a knowledgeable guide.

"You don't seem to have any homeless people around," I observed as we were touring the Kingdom.

"That's because we don't have any, madam," Carlo explained. "The Kingdom takes care of its citizens, and they all have homes."

"It's surrounded by trees, and it's so clean," Sofia commented.

"Environmental responsibility is fostered within the Kingdom, and Marvellans practice it," Carlo added.

I noticed that Marvellans, in general, resemble Italians with their striking features. They are not as fair-skinned as the French and Spanish. We saw a number of good-looking men and women during our tour. We later had dinner at the castle with Franco and his family.

We met for breakfast at the dining room the following morning before our tour. It was a buffet breakfast with a wide array of choices. I whispered to Sofia that this must be how royals have breakfast, and they considered it the important meal of the day. I observed that Franco helped himself to a hearty breakfast. I had an omelet with toast, a sausage, and two cups of coffee. The rest of the royal family joined us, except the grandkids, who left early for school.

We resumed our tour after breakfast, and Sofia went shopping at their crafts market. I bought a bracelet for myself and one for Jesse's wife Christine. Carlo let us try their food during lunch at one of their local restaurants. The cuisine was closely Italian with the usual *pasta* and *pizza* our palates were familiar with in the Philippines, plus other Mediterranean dishes peculiar to the region.

After lunch, Carlo led us to a tour of the vineyard owned by the royal family. We saw the acres of uniformed rows of grapevines. He also showed us the buildings where the wine was processed, which the manager there explained to us in detail. Dinner was our last meal before the wedding. Before dinner, Franco reached for my hand and led me to the library.

"This is our last night before the wedding, my love," looking intently into my eyes. "I can't wait to make you my Queen." I was filled with emotion with the way he said that to me.

"About that. Can I just be your wife, and not Queen?" He raised his eyebrows.

"Don't you want to be my Queen?"

"Actually not the 'Queen' title, but I want to be your wife and partner."

"You truly amaze me, darling. I didn't know that there is such a woman who doesn't want to be Queen. I am under the impression that it's every woman's dream to become a queen or princess."

"I guess that's only in fantasy stories. I love you as you are, whether you're King or not."

"You're something else, and I love you even more for that. Let's not dwell on that subject for the meantime, and just focus on our wedding tomorrow. We can set that aside for further discussion."

He did not seem displeased, but he appeared surprised. We kissed, then he held my hand, and we returned to the dining area. There were always staff who served us our meals while dining in a seating arrangement, just the way I pictured it in "Downton Abbey." There was wine served during meals, and that confirmed that Europeans always have wine with their meals.

Our animated conversations resumed after dinner as we moved to the receiving area. Every time I glanced at Franco from across the room, I found his eyes on me. He gave me his captivating smile, and I smiled back. How can I not love this handsome man who will soon be my husband?

Chapter

2

I woke up with a smile on my face, and I felt exuberant with the powerful stirring of unexplained happiness. This must be how every bride feels on her wedding day. Our wedding was at 10:30 in the morning. We were served breakfast in a smaller dining room on the second floor so I would not run into Franco before the wedding. It seemed that this practice is followed everywhere. We did not have to rush because the chapel was just some short steps away.

I do not normally wear heavy make-up, so I applied my own light make-up. I am blessed with long thick eyelashes, and all I needed was mascara. I planned to wear my hair brushed-up, and Mira, the lady-in-waiting assigned to me, knew how to do my hair. She attached my bridal veil behind my hair bun.

I was thrilled looking at my mirror image, and Sofia was just as thrilled when she saw me in my wedding gown. I looked beautiful. I slowly descended the stairs, bouquet in hand, and I spotted Jesse waiting for me at the bottom. There were just one photographer and one videographer to cover the proceedings, and I learned later that they were part of the castle staff for special events like this. I held on to Jesse's arm, and we walked towards the chapel. The organ played as the door of the chapel opened. I could see Franco at the altar, very attractive and dignified in his King's uniform, smiling at me, and I was elated and nervous at the same time. Today I am marrying my soul mate.

We had a small wedding entourage with Franco's two granddaughters as flower girls in cute identical dresses, and his grandson carrying the pillow with the coins. His son Franz was his best man, and Sofia was my matron-of-honor. As I reached the altar, Franco took my hand and whispered, "You're very beautiful." His statement was enough to make me feel blessed.

We had a Catholic ceremony. The small chapel was adorned with lovely flowers, and their scent permeated the entire area. The castle's regular priest, who usually celebrates Mass there on Sundays, officiated at our ceremony. I was too nervous to remember his name. The chapel was filled to capacity because Franco invited the castle staff too. That is how caring a King he is.

After slipping our wedding rings on each other, we recited our wedding vows, and Franco was the first to speak. We agreed earlier to keep our vows brief. He reached for my hand and kisses it first. Then he held both my hands, and we faced each other as he began,

"My darling Marianne, I fell in love with you the first time I saw you."

I was unprepared with his statement, and I could not help but whisper audibly, "Seriously? At the park?" This was most unusual because the normal vows are never interrupted.

"Yes, at the park. It was a case of love at first sight, and I knew right away that you are the woman for me." I could not believe it, and I just kept quiet. "You are the most beautiful woman I've ever met. You don't draw attention to yourself and you don't even want to be Queen, which we'll discuss later." This brought smiles to the small congregation. "Today you make me the happiest person by becoming my wife. You are the center of my universe, and I need you in my life. It is my ultimate goal to make you happy. I promise to love you every day of my life, my darling."

I gazed at Franco's penetrating deep-blue eyes, which inspired me to say, "Franco, my love, I want to be a good wife to you, and support you in every way as your lifetime partner. It was overwhelming enough to marry a King, and this was not even part of my wildest dreams, but God led you to me, and I thank Him for sending me a wonderful man like you. I must be the luckiest woman in the world, and my heart now bursts with joy. I love you too very much with my very heart and soul."

We kissed to the applause of the congregation, which proceeded to the spacious drawing room for a sumptuous buffet lunch. Everyone congratulated us, including the castle staff who were all present. It was evident how much they love their King. The area was beautifully decorated for the special occasion by the castle staff with an abundance of flowers.

We had a lovely three-tiered cake the pastry chef under Chef Martin created. It was topped with a gold crown to signify Franco's royal stature. Right below it was a spray resembling a fountain cascading below. On the second tier were figures of a sitting bride and groom kissing, and not in the usual standing position. On the bottom tier was an open book to represent the project we were working on together. It had small sugar flowers all over it in pastel colors. The cake itself was delicious. I personally thanked Chef Martin and his staff for their creative handiwork.

My wedding gown attracted much admiration from the royal family and the castle staff. They were all awed by it, especially when they learned that the material and embroidery were all Philippine-made, and they were impressed with the workmanship. Franco himself openly declared I looked utterly radiant, and he admitted he could not keep his eyes off me.

I was gradually getting to know the castle staff, and memorized their names. I wanted to be able to address them by their first names soon. I learned that Mr. Creely, the head butler, was married to the housekeeper, Ms. Ethel. They reminded me of Mr. Carson and Mrs. Hughes in "Downton Abbey," who got married while they were employed there.

It was a lovely wedding in my book, and I had attended hundreds of weddings before. I may be biased too because it was my own wedding, and my groom made it the best one ever. Our reception lasted for several hours. There was much food, and the guests all had their fill. I could barely eat due to my anxious state. Sofia noticed that I was eating very little, and she urged me to take something to nourish me.

"Hey, you need to eat. Remember, you're going on your honeymoon. You need strength and energy, Marianne," she ribbed me.

"Sofia, don't scare me. You can see I'm already nervous as it is."

"Haha. Just enjoy your honeymoon. I'm sure you will. Matteo and I look forward to our extended holiday. Franco's assistant Carlo is very competent. He arranged our trips, including Jesse's flight home tomorrow."

"I'm so happy with how the wedding turned out. Wasn't it lovely?"

"Just perfect. They took care of every detail. Did you see how Franco treats the castle staff? He's such a kind monarch. Marianne, you're going to be very happy with him. Think twice about becoming Queen. You deserve to be Queen, but then you're not after the title."

"He said we'll be discussing it when we return from our honeymoon. Then there's also the announcement he needs to make to the people of Marvella about our unannounced marriage."

* * *

After changing into more casual clothes for our honeymoon trip, I said my goodbyes to Sofia, Matteo, and Jesse. I was somewhat sad not knowing when I would see them again. We can still communicate on Face Time, but face-to-face is different, especially with Sofia.

"You're in good hands, Marianne. King Franco is a great guy," Jesse assured me. "He promised me that he'll take care of you, and I'm happy with that."

"How nice to hear that. Have a safe trip, and say hello to Christine for me. You are always welcome to visit us here." I hugged my only sibling as we said goodbye.

"Christine will surely be shocked when I tell her about your marriage. Wait till she sees the photos I took," he said, smiling.

"Where are you going for your honeymoon?," Sofia asked.

"Franco appears mysterious about it. I know it's somewhere in Italy, but he wants to surprise me. I hope it's Positano because I've always wanted to go there."

"Are you excited?"

"Excited and as nervous as a young bride, which I'm not. I still can't believe I'm now a married woman, Sofia."

"You married the most wonderful man, Marianne, and I know you love him very much. It's indeed worth the wait even if you were not looking for a partner. It's your destiny."

"Thank God for destiny. Wish me luck."

"Good luck, my friend, and have a great honeymoon."

"Thanks, Sofia, and enjoy your holiday with Matteo. Keep in touch."

* * *

"Tell me, Franco, did you really fall in love with me at first sight?"

"Yes, my love. You were so beautiful when you appeared at the park, and I fell in love with your legs too. You have great legs." There went my blush again.

Chapter

3

Franco's driver brought us to nearby Italy. Chef Martin packed for us a portion of our wedding cake in a box to bring along. I realized that security is a major issue among royals. Even on our honeymoon, there were security men in separate vehicles – one in front of us and another one behind us. They are practically inconspicuous when we are in public, but we know they are there. Marvella's provision for security is not as complex as England's, and it is mainly to ensure their monarch's safety. We also use "Morandi" when making hotel bookings as a precaution, and not call attention to Franco's status since few people actually know his surname.

Franco put up the shield separating the driver from the passengers because he did not want his driver to witness us kissing. My husband proceeded to kiss me during the trip. When I caressed his beard, he brought my hand to his lips and kissed it, making me shiver with delight. I found myself responding ardently to his kisses, and I then became fully aware of my great capacity for loving another human being.

He appreciated my wedding gift for him, but I was not prepared for his wedding gift for me. He gifted me a ladies' gold Rolex watch like his, but smaller.

"Franco, this is too expensive," I reacted.

"Don't worry about it. I want us to wear the same watch, so you can discard or give away your other watches."

"I can't believe I'm married. It wasn't even part of my life plan. My parents must be looking down from heaven now, and they can't believe I married a King."

"Well, now you're officially my wife and Queen. There's no escaping from it," he jokingly warned me.

"I promise to always stay by your side, darling," and I was rewarded with a smile.

In-between kisses, I asked him where we were headed for our honeymoon.

"Somewhere in Italy. Take a guess," he dared me.

"I don't have the faintest idea, but there are places I'd love to visit."

"Such as?"

"Well, Positano, for one. It's very enticing in photos."

"That's where we're going. You're a good guesser." He kissed my forehead to indicate that he was impressed with my correct guess.

I jumped in my seat and rained kisses on him. "Oh, I love you, my King." Positano is in the Amalfi Coast of Italy.

"Haha. I guess what you want is also what I want."

It was early evening when we reached Positano. It has a strong romantic allure by the way it is positioned on hilly terrain. Without warning, Franco lifted me up and carried me through the threshold of the bridal suite in the classy hotel with a breath-taking view of the ocean. I rested my head on my husband's shoulder, behaving like a real bride. When he put me down, I just stood at the balcony in awe, admiring the incredible view. Franco hugged me from behind, and dropped a kiss on my neck.

"This is so beautiful," I uttered.

"You're more beautiful". His eyes were on me as I turned my head, and I could not stop the blush from creeping into my face.

"Oh, Franco, you're making me blush again. This is most unusual for a 60-year-old."

"I like it when you blush because it means I touched a tender spot in you."

Aside from the spectacular view from its balcony, the bridal suite was the best in the house with a large bed and an equally large bathroom complete with a Jacuzzi.

"Let's go down and have dinner, shall we? Better start our honeymoon on a full stomach," Franco expressed in jest.

We had seafood dinner at an *al fresco* eatery, and I had no qualms ordering the lobster, and so did he.

"I read somewhere that royals are not allowed to eat shellfish because of the danger of food poisoning. Is this true?" I questioned Franco.

"I've heard that they have such a restriction with the English royals, but as I've said before, we don't impose restrictions in Marvella."

I could not brush aside my feeling of anxiety in anticipation of what was ahead, but I tried to eat as much of what was on my plate and just enjoyed my food.

"Do you snore?" I inquired during dinner, not knowing what to expect.

"No. Do you? It seems important to you," he affirmed with a smile while eyeing me.

I shook my head. "Just curious because that has now become a reason for divorce," I explained.

He laughed. "People concoct alibis for separation. Anyway, I don't favor divorce, and we have no divorce in Marvella, so you're stuck with me, my love." He made me laugh too. I like it when he lowers his head a bit and looks at me fixedly with those penetrating eyes. It is his way of teasing me.

The place had a dance area, and a few couples were dancing to the soft slow music. Franco led me to the dance floor, and we danced locked in each other's arms. It was wonderful being in my loved one's embrace with the music playing.

"You always smell good," he whispered as he drew me closer.

"You too. It's your natural smell that I love," I admitted to him.

* * *

Back in our suite, we had separate baths, which I insisted on because I was still subdued by my shyness, and my considerate and understanding husband acceded.

"How do you feel now, darling?" he asked me afterwards in the most tender tone.

"To tell you frankly, I'm nervous. I have no experience with any man, and I don't want to disappoint you." He pulled me gently into his arms.

"Nothing to be nervous about, my love. You'll never be a disappointment to me. You're a great blessing instead. We'll take it slowly, and I'll be gentle." I remained wrapped in his arms for a long time, and he waited until my nervousness dissipated. His embrace, caresses, and kisses always soothed me.

* * *

I had no words to describe my honeymoon because it was indescribable. If I were to use the proper adjectives, they would all be in the superlative degree. This was prompted by my overpowering love for my husband, and he made me feel that he was just as madly in love with me. I vowed to myself to make our life together an unforgettable existence, considering that we fell in love late in life, so each year is a gift.

It takes getting used to waking up in the morning locked in somebody's arms who is practically a total stranger. We slept embracing or spooning, something totally new to me. I never slept with anybody on the same bed even as a child because I always had my own bed to myself. Even when our cousins came to visit, they were always given their own beds to sleep on in the guest room, and I did not have to share mine with anybody.

The following morning into our honeymoon, I was on the verge of doing an about-face as I encountered a shirtless Franco in the bathroom wearing only boxer shorts with his chest hair exposed, and I was overcome by his sexy image, but he noticed me about to change course.

"Darling, come here," he said, approaching me and taking me into his arms. "Are you embarrassed to see me half-dressed?" He compelled me to look into his eyes.

My hand was touching his chest, and I felt the growth underneath. "Sorry, I'm just not used to it yet." I was conscious of my discomfort. "I'm getting there. Please understand that I've never seen a naked man before."

"I'm your husband now," he voiced. "Don't be embarrassed." He sounded amused with me. "You do have a childlike quality in you, and I admire that. So, I'm your first. No regrets?"

"No regrets. I'm glad you're my first, my last, and my forever."

"I'm honored." He hugged me more.

"In this day and age, I'm indeed a rarity, but I equate sex with love."

"Thank you for loving me, my darling," and he gave me a long kiss.

I like it that he has no tattoo in any part of his body. I do not like tattoos, and I cannot understand why these young people desecrate their bodies. I guess I am old-fashioned. I am happy with my husband's body the way it is. It makes me wonder if other royals have tattoos.

"I'm glad you have no tattoos," I confessed, and he laughed.

"I believe most royals I know don't have tattoos. It doesn't seem to be a royal thing."

In the next days, he introduced me gradually to increased intimacy that I definitely did not want our honeymoon to end. I was completely ecstatic being with Franco, my husband, every minute of the day. I was getting to know love at its very depth. He kindled the dormant embers of my emotions. His full attention was riveted on me from the moment of waking up until sleeping time. What more can I ask for? He practically doted on me. He ensured that I was constantly happy and satisfied. I did not need the title of "Queen" to feel like one with the way he treated me. This King knows how to please a woman, and I happen to be the very lucky one.

After several days into our blissful honeymoon, we walked around quaint Positano one sunny day to explore the area, and marveled at the houses perched on the hills. It was incomparably a very romantic place. We sat on the rocks and faced the ocean, taking in the awesome view. I loved sitting close to him, feeling his body against mine, and encircled in his arms. We also climbed to the top of the hills to get a panoramic view of the ocean and the houses below us.

"I feel like using the Jacuzzi after all that walk today. Will you join me, love?," he suggested.

I hesitated for a second because I still hadn't completely gotten over my shyness. We had showered together, but a Jacuzzi bares everything, yet I was excited about it.

"Okay," I agreed with some reservation. It turned out to be a pleasurable experience I will never forget, and look forward to every time.

I pondered that just over a month ago, he was a complete stranger to me, and now he is my husband and lover. Everything flew so fast that suddenly I found myself married, and to think that I had planned to remain single all my life. I still could not believe meeting, knowing, and marrying such a wonderful man and a King. What had I done to deserve a heaven like this?

I was sad and nostalgic as we were about to leave Positano. I was at my happiest in this place. It will always be paradise to us, our Eden. Franco sensed my sullen state and promised me that we will return to this place on our anniversary every year, or even in-between. He added that it was not far from Marvella, so we could come here anytime.

Chapter

4

Franco swept me off my feet once more as he bodily carried me into his bedroom and quarters as we arrived at the castle. It was larger than any other bedroom in the castle. It had an anteroom, which extended to the wide bedroom with a king-size bed. He is King, so his bed has to be king-size.

"This is huge. You can actually dance in it," I voiced my immediate impression. He momentarily put me down gently, then left my side, and suddenly music floated into the room. Franco extended his hand to me.

"Will you dance with me, lovely lady?" I accepted his hand, and we danced to fox trot music. He was adept at dancing too as he guided me on the bedroom floor, and I was delighted to keep in step with him.

"You keep springing surprises on me," I mentioned to him.

"Don't you love surprises?"

"I do too. Thank you for all the attention you've been giving me. You're practically spoiling me."

"You deserve it, sweetheart. Where have you been all my life?"

"I was going to ask you that very same question."

"I just can't promise to be with you every minute when I'm discharging my duties as King. In the next hour I'll be busy crafting my announcement for the televised coverage tomorrow."

"That's fine. I can even help you edit your announcement if you want."

"I'll have you check the final copy. Okay?"

* * *

I explored the expanse of his bedroom, which was now mine too. It had a wide bathroom with twin vanities and a Jacuzzi. Due to its dimensions, there was no chance of ever bumping into each other. There were separate walk-in closets for us. Compared to his, mine still needed some filling up because I left some of my clothes behind. A fireplace was the main feature of the bedroom.

On one end of the anteroom was a medium-size refrigerator which held cold drinks and water, low-fat ice cream and yoghurt, chocolates, and other eats. On the same end was a round table for four with a large vase of roses on top it, giving off a pleasant aroma, which filled the anteroom. On the other end was a buffet table with our food choices - a tray with more chocolates and our favorite Tootsie Pops, another tray with fresh fruits, and a machine for brewed coffee. The entire wall of that side of the anteroom had tall built-in bookshelves displaying Franco's books. I know that he also reads books from Kindle. My husband is apparently a bookworm. On the same side was a sofa facing a wide-screen flat TV.

Franco has his valet Anton who attends to him and helps him dress up. My lady-in-waiting Mira attends to me too, although I prefer dressing up myself.

"I'm curious. Will I change my name to 'Marianne Morandi'? It does have a nice ring to it," I conveyed to Franco.

"Yes, just for legal purposes, but when you become Queen, you'll be known by another title, and we'll arrange your change of citizenship." I did not say a word because I really did not want to be Queen. "To me, you're still my 'Diez', my perfect '10'." I felt a blush coming on again.

* * *

Franco spent about just an hour in the afternoon writing his announcement on his desk in the bedroom, and I left him by himself. Afterwards, he handed me a piece of paper.

"Darling, this is the draft of my announcement. I'll ask you to go through it before giving it to Carlo for the final copy."

This was the content of his brief announcement:

"Good morning, my people of Marvella. I am making this announcement to share with you a recent very special event in my life, your King's life. I got married to a wonderful woman, whom I know you will love as much as I do. She did not want a lavish wedding, so we had just a simple ceremony in the castle. I consider this the best decision I have ever made. At the moment, my wife does not want to be Queen since she said this is not her reason for accepting my marriage proposal, so that topic still remains in the air. However, I want to introduce her to all of you. We will appear today with my family at the balcony of the Morandi Palace at 5:00 this afternoon. Then my wife and I will go around the Kingdom as my way of introducing her to you. I hope to see you later, people of Marvella."

"It looks okay, but aren't you building me up too much?," I imparted my opinion to Franco.

"I don't think so. I'll have Carlo finalize this, and we can do the broadcast tomorrow morning."

* * *

We woke up at 7:00 a.m. the following morning as Franco's valet Anton entered our bedroom to help him get dressed for the live telecast. The TV crew set up their equipment early in the castle library. Franco was ready and looking resplendent in his uniform before 8:00 a.m., and I swooned privately watching my husband and King from the sidelines. I remained in the room during the live telecast, which began promptly on the dot and aired throughout Marvella. A day before the actual telecast, a rider ran on TV, advising the people to watch out for it.

Franco did not want to appear too formal and sitting at his desk. He preferred instead to casually rest one leg in front of the table, which I thought was more acceptable, while he delivered his announcement. He made a better impact, and I say this not just because I am in love with him. His voice, language, and appearance were just perfect in my judgment.

After the king's announcement was aired on national TV, Carlo and the castle staff gave us feedback gathered within the Kingdom, which was a-buzz of their king's sudden marriage. I became the person of interest, and everyone wanted to catch a glimpse of this woman he fell in love with and married. How could I not feel uneasy with all the attention and curiosity shifted on me? I was apparently concerned that I may not come up to the expectations of the people for their King. Only Franco's assurance and loving gestures calmed me. During such moments, I relied solely on his support. He had always been there for me.

I wore my wedding dress minus the veil with Franco's approval. The Morandi Palace is the seat of the monarchy. It faces an expansive plaza where Marvellans gather for grand occasions. The royal family usually joins the King in the balcony, including the spouses and grandchildren. I observed again the intricate "M" carved or etched on its gates and doors.

We all appeared on the balcony when the clock struck 5:00 p.m. and we were met by an unexpected mammoth crowd, which covered every space of the plaza, cheering loudly. I did not know how to react and just followed the rest of the royal family in waving to the crowd, and getting to master the "celebrity wave".

I knew the crowd's enthusiasm was more for their well-loved King, and I just shared in it. All the while, Franco's arm was draped on my shoulder in an affectionate way. Towards the end, he gave me a kiss on the lips, which pleased the crowd as the cheering became louder without let-up. Our balcony appearance was brief. Then Franco and I proceeded to ride in a horse-drawn open carriage with four white horses, flanked by soldiers garbed in royal blue uniforms with red trimmings and gold buttons on horseback, and wearing plumed headgear. There were four of them in front and four behind us on black horses. The carriage carried us through the streets lined with people cheering us as we passed by, and we smiled and waved at them. It was a rousing reception, and I was astounded with the love Marvellans bestowed on their illustrious King.

Chapter

5

"Wow, that was something," I mentioned to Franco after our balcony appearance. "I can now see clearly how much the people of Marvella love you."

"They will love you too. You'll see."

"You are the quintessential King. I've never witnessed such great love for a King."

"That's a big word to describe me. You're just as important now, so we need to discuss your becoming my Queen. If it's all right with you, you can tell me in the presence of Franz and Tania the reason for your hesitation. They have the right to know how you feel about it. I assure you, no pressure on my part, but you need to have a valid and convincing reason."

I went into his arms. "Darling, I hope I'm not offending you. Okay, I agree to discuss it with you and your children."

We met at tea time the next day, just the four of us, while having tea and scones. I spoke first and confessed to them that I fell in love with Franco not because he is King. It had nothing to do with that because I never wanted to be Queen in the first place. Franz and Tania nodded their heads slightly to indicate that they understood me. I sensed that they believed me, and I could read that they knew I was not after fame and fortune.

I was aware that a prenuptial agreement is usually drawn up when marrying into royalty. In my case, there was never any mention of that. The royal family must have been conscious of the fact that I am rich in my own right, although by Philippine standards. The reality that I am not eager to become Queen is an obvious indication that I am not the ambitious kind, and I have no interest in royal wealth. In my heart, I married purely for love.

Franco never brags about his kingship and assets. I learned through casual conversations that he owns homes in other parts of the world, like New York, London, Paris, Spain, and Scotland, but his possessions are not really important to me. When he talks about them, he always says "we" or "our" as his way of making me part of these, and I am grateful.

"Was there ever an instance in history where the King had a wife, but did not have the title of Queen?" I posed my question to them.

"Not to my knowledge," Franz reacted. "I don't think any woman would refuse such a title."

"We are not aware if there were similar instances in other monarchies, but certainly not in Marvella," Tania disclosed.

"I love your father very much," I expressed, glancing at Franco and touching his hand. "I simply want to be his wife and partner." Franco's eyes were on me, and I could not read his expression.

"Will you be my Queen too?" Franco intercepted. "Is that too hard, my love?"

"Does it mean that much to you?" I challenged him directly.

"Yes, it does," he declared firmly with obvious certainty. "I want my wife to reign beside me as my Queen. You mean the world to me. I don't want it any other way."

I paused for some seconds to ponder on what he just said. He admitted how important my becoming Queen was to him, and he meant a lot to me too. For a brief moment, I was confused, but the realization that I should follow my husband's wish prevailed.

"I love you too much to refuse you, my darling," I enunciated, touching his cheek, and he took my hand and kissed it. His controlling side won me over once more.

"Thank you, sweetheart. You just made me very happy." He beamed and bussed me on the cheek.

* * *

Franco left for the Palace the following morning to attend to business matters. I expected him to be occupied the entire day with work he left behind while he was away. By mid-morning he was suddenly back and entered our bedroom.

"Back so soon? Is everything okay, darling? I inquired.

He rushed to my side and locked me in his arms. "I couldn't concentrate on work. I miss you terribly. *Ti penso ogni giorno.*" The 'missing' part I understood, and I was touched. The Italian phrase sounded romantic, and I asked him to translate.

"It means 'I think of you every day.' How can I work when you constantly invade my thoughts?"

"Aw, that's so sweet of you. I miss you too, my love. You have to teach me Italian."

After a tender moment, he stayed with me in the bedroom until he drifted into sleep. I like watching his handsome face while asleep.

As I became more familiar with my husband's anatomy, and I was no longer shy in his presence, I openly told him how I love his body, eyes, lips, hair, and beard, and he was endlessly pleased. I could not imagine myself being able to articulate my appreciation of Franco's physical assets to him.

* * *

The coronation of a monarch is an important event in every kingdom. Marvella was no exception. It had no Queen for 10 years because Franco did not remarry. I never imagined that my becoming Queen would cause quite a stir or even made the news, not just in Marvella, but extending to other regions as well. Franco wasted no time. He admitted to me that he was afraid I might change my mind. He immediately scheduled my forthcoming coronation, and set the date with the Archbishop of Marvella and the Royal Court.

I would have preferred my coronation as Queen of Marvella to be without much fanfare, but I was in no position to alter tradition. Coronations are normally held at the grand Cathedral of St. Francis with a large attendance. I chose an elegant pale pink gown embellished with exquisite lace of the same color from among the ones sent for my inspection and approval. I wore the ceremonial red royal cape over it as part of the coronation rite.

I dreaded the long walk starting at the entrance of the Cathedral all alone with everyone's eyes on me, but I had no choice. Almost towards the end of my walk, I spotted Franco standing on the right side facing the altar with a pleased expression on his face and a crown on his head. He gave me that fixed look again with the slightly lowered head as if taunting me of my becoming Queen. I was so anxious that I became oblivious of the entire ceremony, and I was not even conscious of what the officiating Archbishop of Marvella proclaimed when he conferred the title of Queen on me and placed the crown on my head. I became aware only when they unanimously hailed me with "Long Live the Queen", which somehow roused me from my stupor. I received the title of Queen Marianne I. I had to get used to this.

After the solemn rites, we removed our heavy crowns and capes. I was still in a daze, and I had a permanent smile plastered on my face. I deduced from conversations with Marvellans that having a Queen was of vital importance to them. I was certain that I needed to make myself useful as the King's partner in running a kingdom, and I still had a lot to learn. I had always loved stories about royalty, and on this very day, I became officially one of them.

The event was covered by national TV and in their newspapers. The news of my coronation was also picked up by the newspapers of other countries. There was one article written about it with the headline, "The Woman who did not want to be Queen". That sent my guarded privacy down the drain. I knew then that I had better chances of guarding it if I just remained in Marvella forever.

The Marvella media is kinder, perhaps because they love and respect their monarch. They do not entertain gossip nor an *expose* of any kind. Marvella is a laid-back and low-key Kingdom, yet Franco's photograph and mine went on sale, plus other items like T-shirts, banners, mugs, and keychains during my coronation. Carlo affirmed that they were selling briskly, and he brought us some samples. I found that amusing. I did not bank on ever becoming a celebrity.

It is different with Franco because he was born into royalty. He lived in a castle all his life. He is used to the adulation of the people. Yet, I constantly marvel at the way he carries himself without any trace of arrogance or feeling of superiority. When he talks to anybody in Marvella, he behaves as their equal, and never imposes his kingship. I am eternally awed by this wonderful man who is King of Marvella and King of my heart as well.

Chapter

6

On our way to our bedroom after the coronation party, Franco stopped at the doorway and addressed me.

"Your Majesty, enter your *boudoir*," bowing, while making a gesture with his arm to make way for me. He was in the mood of teasing me. I poked him in the ribs, and he reacted with an 'Ouch!', and laughed. He was obviously glad that I was finally his Queen.

"How does it feel to be Queen?"

"I don't know. I guess I have to get used to it. What's important to me is being beside my beloved King. That's all that matters," I answered, hugging him.

"You should know that you do make me happy. Are you happy?"

"Very. You need not ask me that because you can see how genuinely happy I am."

"That's all that matters to me too," kissing the top of my head.

"You know, the only thing that will make me unhappy is when I'll discover that you're having an affair," I conveyed to him.

"What are you saying? That's preposterous. Well, then you've nothing to worry about because that's not going to happen. I promise you that I will never be unfaithful to you."

* * *

Our bedroom area was our sanctuary. This was where we communicated and interacted with each other, and we were never short of topics to discuss. On occasions, we played scrabble, a game we both enjoy. He often outscored me, despite my being an Editor, because he is well-educated and is multi-lingual.

The wide-screen TV set was placed at the anteroom, and not inside the King's bedroom, just like how it was in my condo. While watching TV, I questioned Franco why he did not prefer having the TV in the bedroom. I was curious to know his answer to see if we espoused the same reason.

"The bedroom is meant only for two main activities beginning with the letter S," he stressed. "Do you know what they are?"

"Sleep and sex?"

"Right. Don't you believe that? Those two activities should not be interrupted, so a TV has no place in the bedroom."

"I agree with you. May I ask you one more question?

It's quite all right if you don't want to answer it. What was your late wife like?"

He made a deep sigh. Clearly, he did not expect the question. "It's all right to ask me that, darling. She was not like you. I married her because I was under pressure to produce an heir when I became King. She was from a good family in Marvella, but I wasn't in love with her."

"What did she die of?"

"She caught pneumonia and succumbed to it. She didn't take care of herself. She was a cold person, and we never connected. I've known love and happiness only with you."

"Oh, Franco, I love you so. Did you have girlfriends after that? Well, you're a man and you have your needs."

"No, my love. I was celibate. I buried myself in my work and focused all my attention on my responsibilities as King. At the end of the day, I was exhausted and just went to sleep. No woman caught my interest until I met you."

"Aw, you flatter me endlessly."

"Now you know why I have all this boundless energy in our marriage. It's because I've been suppressed for so long," he stated with a smile.

"Well, I'm not complaining," hugging him tighter. "Were you ever tempted to marry again?"

"There were well-meaning efforts to match me with a number of available women, but there was no chemistry. I wanted to fall in love, and with you, it was instant. Do you know that I returned to the park, hoping to run into you?"

"You did?, and I avoided the park after that because I was afraid Khaleesi would embarrass me again. Lo and behold, we met again at the Rosetti condo, and catching you staring at me made me very uncomfortable."

"I couldn't help admiring your beauty."

"Aw. A lot of women must have flirted with you. You're so handsome and you're King."

"Maybe, but I didn't succumb to temptation because of my position as King. I'm a morally responsible Catholic. I could not taint it with a scandal and lose my credibility as a ruler. I owe it to the people."

"You're such a good monarch, and you don't even think of yourself."

"Remember that woman you inquired about at your coronation?"

"The blonde one with the heavy make-up? I wanted to know who she was then because she was giving me dagger looks, especially when you approached me and gave me a kiss."

"She was one of the women they were matching me up with. I opted out after the first date because I found her shallow and uninteresting, but she pursued and stalked me relentlessly. Franz was concerned. He tightened my security detail, providing additional bodyguards around me everywhere I went. She's only in her 50s, but you look younger than she is."

"I'm Asian, and Asians do look younger than Caucasians. How did she pursue and stalk you?"

"Somehow she knew my schedule. She dropped by the Palace unannounced insisting on seeing me, but she didn't succeed because I had tight security. One time I was doing my afternoon walk in the castle grounds with two security staff ahead of me and two behind. I saw her coming towards us at a short distance. The two security staff in front moved quickly, and accosted her, while the other two led me back to the castle. We didn't even know how she managed to get within the castle's perimeter. She was brought to the Palace, and the Royal Court gave her a sentence of a month in jail for harassing the King, which I reduced to a week. She learned her lesson, and never bothered me again."

"How clever of her, but I can't be that aggressive to chase someone who doesn't like me. By the way, darling, I've never seen you angry since I met you. Do you have a temper?"

"Yes, when I was younger. I guess I mellowed a bit when I got older. At Eton, I was even in a fist fight with another prince. I gave him a black-eye, and I got punished for it. Nothing angers me anymore. Now let's talk about you. What do you want to do as Queen? You're not really expected to take on herculean tasks. You can even take it easy and be just a Queen of leisure."

"I don't want to be idle. I want to be useful and productive. Actually, I have a million ideas that I need to organize."

"I'll assign a secretary to assist you. She can help you organize things."

"Thank you. That would be wonderful."

I was playing Frank Sinatra's piece "Strangers in the Night", and then I suddenly wanted to dance. I grabbed Franco's hand.

"Darling, come on, let's dance. This piece sort of describes the nature of our relationship." He was more than willing. We continued to dance for half an hour, and we both enjoyed it, holding each other very close while moving with the music.

"This bedroom is approximately the size of a ballroom. Can we dance more often? I asked.

"Sure. Anytime you want, sweetheart." It is a wonderful way to cap the day in each other's arms and dancing to music.

* * *

Franco is a fast-acting King. The following day, Lola, who was in her early 30s, reported to me as my secretary. She had a pleasant disposition and the willingness to work. I had many plans in my head which I discussed with her. She listed them down, then we buckled down to put the items into priority.

I planned to set up a book club, a green club, a crafts class, and a tree planting activity, among other things, for starters. I believed that we should start with the green club for planting vegetables, so the families could soon gain from it. The wide expanse of the castle grounds had countless possibilities. I asked the King's permission to give us an area for the planting which could be divided individually among those interested to develop them.

First, I issued a circular throughout the Kingdom for those who wanted to sign up for the projects. I did it simultaneously with the book club and the crafts class. With the help of Lola, we looked for persons with the competence to handle the crafts sessions. Sergio, the royal gardener, helped us set up the green club and offered pointers to the plot owners on how to raise different vegetables. He had been in-charge of the castle's flower and vegetable gardens for many years. All materials were shouldered by the Kingdom. I handled the book club myself.

In the book club, I assigned a book for the members to read within a month's time. We attracted 15 women to sign up, and we met for the first time in the castle library. I was still not comfortable with being addressed as "Your Majesty", so I told the book club members to address me plainly as "Marianne" within the confines of the library.

I was reading from a passage in the assigned book to the women to get their views on it when I heard the door open and the familiar deep voice that I love. The women all stood up and bowed as the King walked in and approached me.

"Ladies, please remain seated. Sorry to interrupt. I'll just say something to my wife," he explained. He bent down to give me a kiss, then whispered to ask if I was free at 5:30 p.m. to introduce me to an important official.

"We'll be finished at 5:00 p.m., so it's okay," I responded.

"Great. I'll wait for you at the foyer, darling. Love you." He kissed me again.

"Love you too," I whispered.

"Goodbye, ladies," he addressed the group, then he exited the library. The ladies could not contain their excitement.

"Marianne, is he always this sweet?," one of them inquired.

"Always," I confirmed. They swooned in unison, and I learned from them later that many of them had a crush on him.

One of the ladies posed a question to me. "Is it true that you didn't want to be Queen?"

"That's correct," I affirmed.

"But why? That's something every woman dreams of," another pursued the question.

"Okay, I'll tell you my story. I had a comfortable life in my country, I had everything I wanted, and I was happy being single. I thought I didn't need a man in my life because I hadn't fallen in love with anybody. Then I met Franco, and he changed all that. It was a whirlwind courtship. He swept me off my feet, and I fell in love with him. What woman wouldn't fall in love with him? After we got married, I told him that I didn't want the title of Queen because that was not my reason for marrying him, and I am not after fame and fortune, but he wouldn't hear of it. He has an obstinate side too, and he won me over because I love him deeply.

Anyway, continue to call me Marianne within our book club, okay?"

"Wow, it's like a fairy tale," one of them commented. "Thanks for sharing, Marianne."

* * *

The green garden was set up at the periphery of the castle grounds, and a tall fence was constructed around it to discourage animals, like deer that roam the property, to eat the vegetables. Sergio divided it into several individual plots and guided their owners on how to plant and care for the various vegetables. After a month, it was already harvest time for some plants. The owners could choose to either consume their harvests or sell them at the produce market.

Lola found two crafts supervisors. One taught the members to crochet and knit, while the other one handled the quilting, and embroidery sessions. They were able to produce attractive table runners, table cloth, seat covers, baby items, shirts, blouses, and bedcovers. I joined them in the quilting session because I wanted to learn how to make bedcovers and tapestries for my own purpose.

Their products were displayed and sold at the weekend market and during the big semi-annual Country Fair, where Marvellans sell their livestock, farm animals, products, and produce. This major event attracts hundreds of visitors from nearby countries.

The women welcomed the extra money earned from what they produced. The green and crafts projects were part of my Livelihood program. The purpose of the book club was to hone their knowledge and to enhance their learning experience. We had only women in these projects because the men were occupied with running their own businesses, and some were employed in companies. I knew that being Queen was not exactly a soft job. There were myriad projects I wanted to pursue, and just conceptualizing and planning them fired me with enthusiasm.

Chapter

7

It had been a month since my wedding. I decided to communicate with Sofia on Face Time. I had so much to share with her. She shrieked when she saw me online.

"Marianne, how nice to finally see you and talk to you. How was the honeymoon? Are you happy?"

"A big 'yes' to your last question. It was fantastic and beyond my imagination. Hey, friend, it may not be safe to talk about personal matters online. I'm still careful about privacy, more for my husband's sake. That's why I'm not mentioning his name and yours. Why don't we speak in Cebuano, our common dialect?"

"Good idea. I'm so excited to know the details."

We proceeded to talk in our dialect, and I told her in detail about my remarkable honeymoon and what I had been doing.

"It was more than I expected or ever dreamt of. *Ang akong bana buotan nga tawo ug sobra ka cariñoso.*" (My husband is a good man and is very loving).

"I told you so. That's what Matteo said."

"Virile *kaayo siya*" (He's very virile). Then I followed this with "*Unsay* virile *sa atong sinulti-an?*" (What is 'virile' in our dialect?). We had a good laugh at this because we did not know the equivalent of the word.

She was thrilled to hear my stories. We agreed to communicate regularly to keep us abreast of each other's lives.

"So you finally agreed to be Queen. I would have wanted to witness your coronation," Sofia expressed.

"It was a grand ceremony held at the Cathedral. I would have preferred a simpler one, but I could not break protocol. It made my partner very happy when I agreed to become his Queen, and I'm happy too when he is. I can make my own contributions here, so I initiated projects I conceptualized which keep me in touch with the people, but I also have a lot to learn. I find pleasure in learning about royal life. Oh, it's a new and wonderful life, and I'm enjoying it immensely. My man is very supportive and loving."

"I'm happy for you. It's a life you deserve. Fairy tales do happen, huh? Who would have thought that a woman of our age can still find love and happiness?, and you weren't even looking."

"I know. It's meant to be. This guy is indeed God-sent."

* * *

Since moving to Marvella, I limited my use of social media to play safe. I did not use Facebook anymore since I met Franco. We were discreet in our communication. We communicated only through Viber using our iPads, and rarely by phone or text, although in Marvella, people do not eavesdrop nor hack accounts. I still used Face Time with Sofia, but we were extra careful, and we communicated in our dialect. In reality, it is indeed possible to curtail social media exposure. I valued more my face-to-face encounters with Franco.

* * *

My activities were mostly tied up with Franco's. We went riding together, played some tennis, went walking hand-in-hand, visited the gym regularly, and had our painting sessions. He initiated me into golf too. I witnessed him fencing, and it reminded me of the swashbuckling movies I watched in my youth which ushered me to the days of kings and musketeers of yore. The sport certainly had an art of its own. He was also adept at archery.

We visited the royal stables, and he picked a gentle female Palomino named Caramel for me to ride because I was still in the re-learning stage of riding. We also made regular visits to the dog kennels to see Khaleesi and his other dogs. Khaleesi seemed happy where she was, and she was excited to see us every time. One favorite activity we shared was walking along the seashore holding hands and barefoot. I loved beachcombing and picking up seashells. Of course, there were always security staff around us, but we frolicked, kissed, and hugged anyway, and they did not mind us. If we were in another Kingdom, like England, we would surely be tailed by *paparazzi* with their zoom lens. Franco's strategy of keeping a low profile serves its purpose, and he does not attract publicity nor make the news like other monarchs.

Franco and I had so much in common, and we shared the same interests. Sometimes I would ask myself, how is it possible that there is someone like this of my same mold? There was undeniable chemistry between us. To think that we even grew up and lived under different cultures. This must be what being soul mates meant.

"Are you happy?", Franco probed me again one night. This was a question he asked me constantly.

"I've told you that I'm very happy with you, and that's not going to change," I replied. "It's just that…"

He was quick to interrupt me. "Oops, when there's a hint of a 'but', it means that there's something missing. Be honest with me, darling."

"I was just going to tell you that I'd really be happier taking care of you and attending to your needs."

"You're already doing that, my love. You make me extremely happy every day."

"Not exactly. There are people doing things for you who look after your clothes, dress you up, attend to your schedule, cook your food, etc."

"Those are expected in a King's life. We all have roles to play, and those are their roles. They are there to serve their King."

"I know, but as your wife, I want to take care of you."

"Sweetheart, I don't want to burden you with those. You are my Queen, not my servant."

"Allow me to explain. It's normal practice for an Asian woman to take care of her man. It doesn't mean she's subordinate to him. She's still his equal, and not subservient to him. It's done out of love. I want to take care of you, Franco."

"I understand you. I'll make you a compromise. We can spend some time at the royal lakeside cottage, and perhaps you can attend to me there and cook for me. Do you like to cook?"

"I do too. I love you and I want to do things for you. My world revolves around you now."

"Thank you for loving me that much. You overwhelm me." He hugged me. "There's a holiday coming soon, and we can spend it there."

"Can we bring along your grandkids? You haven't spent much time with them lately."

"I like your suggestion. It would be nice to spend some time with them."

* * *

We spent the holiday weekend at the lakeside cottage with his grandkids Francesco (11) and Olivia (8), Franz' kids, and Bianca (7), Tania's daughter. They are such good-looking and well-behaved children. I have not discovered if I have any motherly instinct because I do not have a child of my own, so I was surprised that I connected well with his grandkids.

We still brought along with us his driver, two bodyguards, a nanny to look after the grandkids' needs, and a cook to help me prepare the food. The cottage also had an in-house caretaker who cleaned the place and trimmed the surroundings. We traveled in two vehicles. Before our trip, I listed down the ingredients I would need, and arranged to have them delivered to the castle. The cottage he spoke of was, in fact, a large house with six bedrooms and six bathrooms, and remote-controlled gates.

Franco and the kids had fun swimming in the cool lake for hours. We also went fishing and grilled the fish we caught. I busied myself cooking the recipes I had planned, including desserts. They loved my pasta dishes and my chocolate cake. The appreciation for my cooking from Franco and the kids was heart-warming. In the evening after dinner, we played all sorts of games. I observed that Franco was a loving and concerned grandfather, and he must have been a good father too to Franz and Tania.

His grandkids called him "*Nonno*," which was Italian for "grandfather." Then they started calling me "*Nonna*," which was Italian for "grandmother", and it pleased me.

"Darling, thank you for cooking for me and my grandkids. I enjoyed the food very much, but we can do this only occasionally, otherwise you'll have a fat King," Franco enunciated. I laughed.

"Even if you'll get fat, I'll still love you." It was his turn to laugh.

"In the castle, you notice that our chef cooks only healthy food for us, usually low-fat. I'll need to spend more time in the gym and walk off the pounds I probably gained during this holiday. I also appreciate the other things you've been doing for me, like preparing my clothes, taking care of me, and even giving me massages."

"It was a real pleasure doing those things for the man I love."

Occasionally, I cooked for Franco Filipino dishes I was familiar with, like *sinigang* (a sour soup), *adobo*, and *puchero*. The last two are meat dishes with Spanish influences, and all three are considered healthy food. I shared the recipes with Chef Martin, so sometimes he served them to us. I told Franco jokingly that I was trying to "Filipinize" him, and he found this funny. I have yet to introduce him to *balut* (duck embryo) and *dinuguan* (a blood dish). Although he had tried all sorts of dishes in his trips around the world, he may not be ready for these yet.

* * *

Franco's concern for my well-being never waned. He constantly checked how I was doing, and if I was happy. I developed a slight cough upon our return from our holiday, maybe because it was colder at the lake area. I rarely get sick, except for occasional cough and cold. I tried to put distance between Franco and me because I did not want him to catch my cough, and cautioned him not to kiss me. The King cannot be sick.

He summoned the doctor to look at me. The doctor made his house call at the castle, and he prescribed a cough medicine, but not antibiotics because his diagnosis was that it was not serious. After two days, Franco could not control himself any longer and unexpectedly kissed me long on the lips.

"Darling, why did you do that? You CAN'T get sick. You're King," I stressed to him.

"I don't care. I can't stand not kissing you, and I'll take my chances." He threw me a smile like a little boy caught in a mischief, and I just sighed.

I was worried about his health and I made sure he had plenty of Vitamin C to keep him strong enough to fight the virus. My King exhibited his stubborn side, which I recently discovered. There may still be other traits to discover later.

Chapter

8

As Franco and I were going down the stairs for breakfast, I noticed new photos hanging on the wall along the stairway, where the royal family photos were on display. They were our wedding photos.

"Do you like them?" he asked me, while I inspected them.

"Yes, of course. These are new. It makes me feel really part of your family."

"Darling, you are family. Don't you forget that."

At the breakfast table, the servant placed a glass of smoothie in front of Franco. He took a sip.

"Hey, this is good. It tastes like a mixture of different berries. Here, darling, try this." He offered his glass to me.

"Are you okay with my drinking from your glass?", I reacted.

"Sure. There's nothing wrong with that."

"I'm just thinking that maybe it's not considered appropriate with royalty, or some people may frown at the intimacy of drinking from the same glass."

"Oh, come on, sweetheart, we've indulged in French kissing. That's even more intimate. Unless, of course, you're over-fastidious about it."

"No. I'm perfectly fine with it." I took a sip and I liked it. Just then the servant brought me a glass of the delightful smoothie.

* * *

I always had this desire to learn other languages. I told Franco that I wanted to learn Italian. It would come as an advantage for me since it is Marvella's common tongue. He was willing to teach me. We started with simple greetings and responses like:

Como stai?	How are you?
Buon giorno	Good morning
Buon pomeriggio	Good afternoon
Buona sera	Good evening
Buona notte	Good night
Grazie	Thank you
Molte grazie	Many thanks
Grazie mille	Thanks a lot
Arrivederci	Goodbye
Ciao	Hello
Prego	You're welcome

I practiced these with my husband and the castle staff. Franco was delighted at my enthusiasm to learn Italian. He smiled every time I greeted him in Italian. He uttered these sentences to me often:

Ti amo molto	I love you very much
Sei bellisima	You are very beautiful
Sono attratto	I am attracted to you

Once before leaving the castle, he said to me, "*Dammi un bacio*," and I understood from his gesture that he wanted me to kiss him. I tiptoed because he towered over me, and I kissed him on the lips, which pleased him. Then I told him, "*Arrivederci*," and he smiled at me. Upon his return, he announced, "*Sei la mia anima gemella*," which I did not understand.

"It means 'You are my soul mate,'" he translated. I found it sweet. I considered Italian to be a very romantic language.

"To fully express my love for you, I'll say it in different ways." He then proceeded, "*Te amo* in Spanish, *ti amo*, in Italian, *eu te amo* in Portuguese, and *je t'aime* in French."

"I'm impressed. Why do most royals have the facility for other languages?"

"We have language coaches to expose us to other languages. My grandkids are getting regular lessons."

Franco was my personal teacher, and I was a conscientious student. I also listened to recordings in

Italian. I made a lot of progress, and my sentences got longer in time.

"*Sei il grande amore della mia vita*" (You are the love of my life), I said to him. He was so impressed with my progress that he hugged me tightly.

He responded with "*Voglio passare il resto della mia vita con te*" (I want to spend the rest of my life with you).

"*Voglio invecchiare con te*" (I want to grow old with you), I added, and that made him jubilant.

"You're a fast learner. Listening to you speak Italian pleases me much. The most effective way to learn a language is simply to speak it. You're on the right track, sweetheart."

The language in Marvella is predominantly Italian, and it is the accepted street language. However, British English is also widely spoken, and is the medium of instruction in their schools. The monarchy's mode of communication is English when issuing announcements to the people of Marvella. Franco speaks English with the British accent, and he speaks Italian like a native.

* * *

I continued to discover the nuances of living a royal life. Franco passed on to me a schedule for our portrait paintings. As King and Queen, our portraits had to be on display at the Palace and at the castle. A well-known portrait artist in the Kingdom was commissioned to do our portraits. To my knowledge, you had to pose for one, and somehow I did not favor the long hours of posing for a portrait. I was therefore relieved upon learning that a professional photographer would first take our photos, and the portrait artist would work from these, so that eliminated the awkward moments of keeping still for him while he painted us. If I were in the Philippines, I would not think of having my portrait done.

The professional photographer came to the castle to take our photos. Mira prepared me by fixing my hair and fussing with my gown. Again, I put on light make-up. I wore my elegant coronation gown, and Franco was in his royal uniform. I always admire him in this attire, and he appeared as the eminent King that he is. The several shots taken were turned over to the portrait artist. Before that, Franco and I got to see the photos, and we were pleased with how beautifully they came out. The artist worked on our portraits for a whole month, and indeed he did justice to them too. The paintings came out remarkably life-like. Franco was his handsome kingly self, and I did appear beautiful and queenly.

The unveiling of our portraits was marked by an unostentatious ceremony at the Palace, and Franco got his preference of keeping it simple with just the members of the Royal Court, the Morandi family, and a select few present. Our individual portraits occupied a place of prominence at the Palace. Franco allowed the event to be carried in the local news mainly for the information of the people in the Kingdom. When it became common knowledge that our portraits were on display at the Palace, people came to view and admire them. At the castle's receiving area hung just one portrait of the two of us. I was sitting on a chair, and Franco was standing next to me with his arm resting on the back of my chair. I preferred this one because it was more personal, and it captured us together.

Chapter

9

"Do you miss home?", Franco was prying. He was often concerned about my well-being and wanted to be assured that I was okay. How can I not be touched?

"Not really. This is my home now with you. Of course, sometimes I miss the Filipino food and delicacies, but that's not important because I can still prepare most of them here if I want to with the right ingredients. You are more important to me. I do miss the movies though."

"What movies?"

"As a senior citizen, I get to watch movies for free in Makati. I'm a movie buff, and I like watching on the big screen."

"Darling, the castle has a small theater, so you can still watch movies."

"I didn't know that. Where is it?" The castle was so enormous that there were rooms I had yet to explore.

"I'll take you there. You can tell me what particular movies you want to watch, and we can watch them together. I like watching movies too, and I haven't done that lately. My grandkids often watch children's films."

Franco showed me the theater in the castle which had a seating capacity for 20 viewers. We watched a Hugh Jackman flick one afternoon. We both liked this actor. We had popcorn and orange juice like in a regular cinema. Back home, I sometimes had soda with my popcorn, but soda is discouraged in the castle, and they do not want the kids to get used to it. Thereafter, we made it a regular practice to watch a movie at least once a week, or sometimes twice a week if our schedules allowed it. We practically appreciated the same types of movies, then we discussed the films after viewing, and shared our impressions. He got amused when I cried during touching scenes in the movies, and he ribbed me about it, but at the same time, he comforted me.

I have this habitual reaction of uttering "*Hala ka*" when I am surprised or confused about something occurring unexpectedly. It is a common expression in the Cebuano dialect which has no exact translation. I often reacted using this particular expression when we were watching movies. Franco noticed this, and he asked me what it meant. I explained to him that I did not know how to translate it. The closest equivalent I could think of was "Oh, no", when one was in a quandary. We were watching the evening news in the anteroom after dinner when the news anchor reported that there was a strong earthquake in South America.

"*Hala ka!*," Franco unexpectedly uttered. I burst out laughing.

"You can speak my dialect, and it's the proper reaction too," I said. I continued to giggle.

"Darling, you're laughing at me," my husband accused me with a hint of a frown.

"No, love, I'm not laughing at you. I'm simply amused with you. You can be funny, you know. Hearing you speak my dialect is pure joy." I added, "*Aguy, Dong*, you're so cute," kissing him on the cheek to convince him. ("*Aguy*" is another Cebuano expression, and "*Dong*" is a nickname, which can also be a form of endearment, for a male person).

The next time Sofia and I talked on Face Time, I related to her the *Hala ka* incident, and she could not stop laughing. She found it cute too.

* * *

"Are there areas in the castle which I have yet to explore?" I queried the King.

"I suppose you haven't been to the indoor pool yet?"

"No, not yet. Where is it?"

"It's next to the gym. It's more private compared to the gym. It's for the exclusive use of the family. Let me know when you want to go swimming."

Wonders never ceased. I had not seen yet every nook and cranny of the castle due to its sheer size. We added swimming to our many activities. Sometimes we included his grandkids. They all swim well because they had swimming lessons. I learned how to swim when I was a young girl because my family lived near the ocean, but unlike Franco, I could do only freestyle. He showed me how to do the breast, back, and butterfly strokes. Being married to this King is a continuous learning adventure. Had I opted to remain in my home country, I would be doing the same things, and my life would be at a standstill. My King expanded my horizons beyond my imagination.

The covered tennis court, where we also played earlier, was next to the gym. He made a promise to teach me golf.

"I can only putt. I need to practice my drive,"

"It's a date then."

I could see that I had no reason ever to get bored because there were boundless possibilities of keeping boredom at bay.

My favorite spot, aside from our bedroom, was the *gazebo*, which was outside the main castle within the grounds. This was where I spent my time when Franco was away at work. I read and quilted in this cool and tranquil place. He knew exactly where to find me when I was not in our bedroom. Sometimes Olivia and Bianca joined me in the *gazebo* with their coloring books, and we colored together. One afternoon, Franco chanced upon us concentrated on our coloring, and he was pleased that I was interacting with his granddaughters. I loved the *gazebo* with its hanging flowering plants.

* * *

It was our habit to read in bed and solve crossword puzzles before retiring or indulging in romance. We sometimes talked in-between these.

"I read that public display of affection is not allowed among the British royal family. I notice that William and Kate don't even hold hands in public. Are there restrictions in Marvella? I want to be sure I'm doing things correctly here," I mentioned to Franco.

"No, not here. We can touch, kiss, and hug in public. I don't see anything wrong with that, and I don't like suppressing feelings."

"I'm so glad because I like touching you." He smiled at what I said. "By the way, love, do you have a bucket list?"

"Why, do you have one?"

"Yes, I do. There are places I want to visit and certain events I want to experience. Oh, I suppose you don't have one because you've already been all over the world. So far, I've been to Europe and the US, I've seen Niagara Falls in Canada, Marina Bay Sands in Singapore, and the various beautiful Philippine spots."

"What else are on your list?"

"I want to watch the *aurora borealis* from an igloo in Finland, the Taj Mahal in India, the pools of Pamukkale, and the Burj Khalifa in Dubai. I also want to go up on a hot-air balloon."

"I haven't been on a hot-air balloon myself. That should be exciting. I want to enjoy these places with you, so let's make plans."

* * *

Franco's birthday was on August 1 when he turned 65. He was a typical Leo with a strong personality, domineering, and controlling, but I had no complaints because he was always a gentle and loving husband to me. A month before his birthday, I asked Sofia to get me a gold crucifix with chain as my gift for my husband. She sent me by Messenger some samples to choose from, and I picked something masculine, elegant, and not too fancy. Being married to a man who had everything was no joke. How much more with a King. He was pleased when I presented him with my birthday gift after greeting him with a meaningful kiss.

"Happy Birthday, love. My goodness, you definitely don't look your age."

"Thanks for the compliment, darling. You didn't have to give me a gift," he stated as he slipped the chain with the crucifix over his neck.

"It wasn't easy to find the right gift for someone who already has everything."

"Thank you, sweetheart. I'll wear this all the time," patting the necklace.

"You're the hardest person to buy a gift for. You don't need anything anymore."

"Next time, don't give me anything. It's all right. Don't trouble yourself."

It was the perfect gift after discovering that he was a spiritual person. Earlier, while checking the pockets of his pants when he changed his clothes, I found a rosary inside. I usually like smelling his clothes when he discarded them because they smelled of him, and I loved his natural scent.

"Do you always carry a rosary in your pocket?" I probed.

"Yes, since I was a boy. I received that from the Pope when my father and I visited the Vatican, and I've been praying with it since then."

"I've never seen you pray the rosary."

"That's because I pray in private every day in my office or in the library." I admired him more for that.

* * *

The King's birthday was a festive holiday in Marvella. The holiday was known as The King's Day. People joined or watched the parade around the Kingdom with soldiers in uniform and people wearing the costumes of their trades. Marvella had soldiers, and their male citizens underwent a national service training as a requirement even if they never go to war. The King and Queen rode around in an open carriage to greet the people, waving to admiring crowds lining the streets. I experienced such a festivity beside Franco.

The plaza was transformed into a mini fair, and there were food and drinks for everyone. I joined Franco in mingling with the crowd at the plaza. The people were enthusiastic to see and talk to him, and I was drawn into the frenzy. He was indeed the people's King and an excellent ruler. His popularity equaled, or even surpassed that of a movie star. He held on to my hand as we moved in the crowd, and he introduced me to everybody, saying "This is my wife, your Queen." The people cheered us with *"Lunga vita al re e alla regina"* (Long live the King and Queen).

Even if there were no untoward incidents in Marvella, we were always surrounded by security men when we moved among the crowd. I guess this is normal in every monarchy. I was received warmly by the people, and they were all eager to shake my hand. A grandmother approached me and said, *"Molto bella"* (very beautiful), referring to me, and I thanked her and shook her hand. I had my day of fame. The King's Day culminated with a magnificent fireworks display, which the royal family witnessed from the Palace balcony.

In the Philippines, it is a common practice for people to take selfies with their cellphones. Everyone does it, but not in Marvella. They are not slaves to their cellphones, and taking photos of their monarchs is not something you see them do, borne out of respect.

"Darling, when my birthday comes, is it all right if we don't have a Queen's Day?"

"Is that what you want? We did have such an occasion before."

"Yes. I don't want to draw attention to myself. Maybe we can just celebrate it quietly with the family. A King's Day is really appropriate because you're Marvella's rightful monarch."

"Okay. Your wish is my command, my love. You continue to surprise me."

Chapter

10

Franco and I walked to the stables one afternoon to go riding. I was waiting for the stable hand to bring out my horse Caramel, and Franco was about to mount the horse brought out for him. His left foot was on the stirrup when the horse suddenly reared and threw him to the ground. The stable hands rushed to control the horse and pulled it away from Franco.

"Franco!", I screamed. I ran to where he was lying on the ground. He appeared to be in pain. I held his hand. I was devastated. He is my world, and I could not bear to see him in pain. Carlo was there with us as it happened, and he immediately called for an ambulance. I instructed everyone there not to move the King until the ambulance arrived. My late father was a doctor and I learned a few things from him about accidents.

I requested them to give me something to put under Franco's head to keep him comfortable, and someone handed me a folded blanket. The ambulance responded in just a few minutes, and Carlo and I rode in the ambulance with Franco to the hospital after the paramedics carefully lifted him to a gurney. Carlo also called Franz and Tania to advise them of the accident. I cried in the ambulance, but hid my tears from Franco.

The hospital personnel panicked when they learned that it was their King who was being brought in. The bone specialist immediately rushed in and ordered an x-ray of the King's leg. Franco was immediately wheeled into the x-ray room, while Carlo and I waited anxiously outside.

The doctor emerged afterwards and told us that Franco had a slight fracture in his leg, which would not require surgery, but it had to be put in a cast. He needed at least a few days of confinement for it. He showed us the film of the x-ray. When Franz and Tania arrived, we apprised them of Franco's condition.

The doctor put his injured leg in a cast. Franco was not happy about his confinement, so I tried my best to comfort him. I remained with him in the hospital because he did not want me to leave his side. He was assigned a large suite fit for a king. News of his accident spread throughout the Kingdom and was carried in the news. He could not receive visitors, apart from his immediate family, but flowers, food, and cards poured in from those concerned about him and were praying for him.

He is an active person, so confinement puts limitations on his normal movements. When he learned from the doctor that his cast would stay for several weeks, he was more depressed, and I continued to give him the TLC he needed badly. It was all I could do to diffuse his restlessness and discontent. I had never been as attentive and loving towards him as at this time.

On the second day of his confinement, the grandkids came to visit, and Franco was glad to see them. Upon entering his room, Bianca started to cry when she saw her grandfather lying in bed.

"*Nonno, ti amo,*" shedding copious tears. She rushed to his bedside to hug him, and Francesco and Olivia followed.

"*Nonno*, will you be able to walk again?", Francesco questioned with worry written on his face.

"Of course, Francesco. I'll recover from this accident."

"Papa, no more riding please," Franz warned him.

"How can I ride in my condition?" Franco sounded sarcastic. He must have felt defeated, and this kind of reaction was not his natural self. "We just have to pick the right horse. I want you to do that when the kids start riding. That particular horse was somewhat agitated, and it wasn't my regular polo horse. I may not ride for the meantime when I'm up and about until I get past the trauma of this unfortunate incident."

* * *

The King returned home to the castle with his leg in a cast. From the car, he was transferred to a wheelchair. The castle has an elevator, which is rarely used, and he was transported upstairs using it. He also used a crutch to walk by himself, and he refused to be assisted. A male nurse attended to him in at least administering his medicines.

I acted as his personal nurse, and I did not mind looking after him. He was not exactly a difficult patient, but he depended much on me and did not want me out of his sight. I did not know if I should be flattered, but I love him too much to really mind. I aided him in his bathroom trips and in getting on our bed. Our meals were served in the anteroom so we did not have to go downstairs, but I fed him breakfast in bed. When were are not watching TV in the anteroom, where a special chair was set up for him with an ottoman to rest his leg, we remained in bed with me cuddling him. Somehow it comforted him.

He lost his smile in his physical condition. The rare times when he smiled were during the visits from his grandkids. They would climb into our bed and shared their stories with him, and he would momentarily look happy in their presence. He did not want them to see him sad.

I put up a pleasant front for him, and tried to coax him to smile, and sometimes I succeeded. When his hair appeared tousled, I brushed it, then kissed him when I was done, telling him "*amore mio*" or "*palangga*" ("beloved" in Italian and Cebuano, respectively). I was rewarded with a hint of a smile, also when I told him "*sei molto bello*" (You are very handsome). I also hugged him a lot to assure him that I was there for him no matter what happens.

Franco continued to work even if he could not be physically present at the workplace, and he communicated with the Palace by phone. Carlo updated him regularly of activities in the Kingdom, coming to our bedroom every morning to deliver his report. The King was used to being active. Thus, inaction was not part of his vocabulary.

Chapter

11

When Sofia and I chatted online again, I shared with her the accounts of Franco's accident.

"That's sad news. How are you faring?" She was shocked to learn about it, and was concerned about my well-being.

"I'm doing all right. He's not really a bad patient, but he's unhappy with his condition, and it pains me seeing him like that."

"I'll pray for his quick recovery. Don't worry, he'll soon be back on his feet. He's strong and healthy."

"I hope so. Thanks for your prayers."

"I was going to share with you a bit of good news."

"What is it?"

"Matteo will be retiring this year. We've decided to move to Marvella and retire there." She clapped her hands with glee.

"That's the best news I've heard so far. That means we'll be seeing more of each other. I can't wait."

"Me too. Noelle is happy about it because she'll be enrolling in College in Europe. Hey, is there anything you need while I'm still here which I can bring you?"

"If it's not much trouble for you, can you bring me *mango* seeds which I can plant here? I miss it, and I also want to set up an orchard here."

"Why not? I'll try to gather the seeds for you."

"Thanks, Sofia. I await your living here permanently with much anticipation."

I also shared with her the events of The King's Day. She enjoyed listening to my stories, and she looked forward to witnessing such events herself.

I related to Franco Matteo's retirement plans. He was glad to know that I would have my best friend nearby when they would eventually move to Marvella. He thought that Matteo may be qualified to fill up a position in the Royal Court. One of the members plans to retire permanently as he turns 75.

* * *

When Franco's leg cast was finally removed, his disposition changed drastically, and he was in high spirits. The doctor reported that his leg healed well after another x-ray was taken to confirm it, and assured him that it was as good as new. It pleased him to know that he could now resume his normal activities.

He could already take the castle stairs easily. He was coming down the long flight of stairs and advancing towards me, while I watched him with pure admiration as he was walking.

"I always love watching you walk," I admitted to him. "You're so sexy, straight, and regal."

"I think I like the sexy part, coming from you."

"You undoubtedly walk like a King."

"I didn't know there's a King's walk. I've always walked like this all my life."

"I like it, and I'll keep watching you walk. Do you feel completely well? How's your leg?"

"My leg is just fine. The doctor said I can resume my normal functions. You know what that means?" He exhibited a naughty expression and winked at me, sending my heart racing. We had been married for several months, but his effect on me had not lost its potency.

"I'm intrigued." We were back to kidding each other again. I liked him in this kind of mood.

"Come here." He enfolded me in his arms. "I don't know how to thank you for all that you have done for me when I was practically immobile."

"It's simply my role as your wife. I like taking care of you because I love you."

"Thank you for loving me. Now that I've recovered, maybe we can start pursuing your bucket list." My face lit up.

"Seriously? Don't you want to start working on your book?"

"That can come later. There's really no hurry, and I didn't set a date for its completion. I'm more inclined to travel with you to Finland and view the *aurora borealis*. You need to be rewarded for being such a perfect wife."

My excitement escalated. This was something I had long wanted to witness.

Chapter

12

Franco did not lose time in making the arrangements for our trip. Carlo assisted us in making the necessary bookings. I needed to do some shopping. I had not done any shopping at all in Marvella because I rarely went out. I resorted to online shopping for warm clothing and the proper pair of boots to wear for our trip. My orders were delivered in a couple of days.

The Northern Lights or *aurora borealis* are best viewed in Finland starting late August. During our booking discussion with Carlo, Franco planned to reserve a suite, but I convinced him that an igloo for two with a bathroom is just right for us, and we did not need fancy accommodations for a few days' stay.

Franco had already witnessed the Northern Lights before, but in Iceland, not from an igloo in Finland. The place in Finland is Kakslauttanen, which is in the wilderness of Lapland. We landed in Ivalo Airport, then we boarded the 30-minute shuttle. We found ourselves in an arctic igloo, which offered unrestricted overhead visibility.

The weather did not disappoint us. We were accorded an astounding performance of dazzling lights in green, pink, and violet across the night sky right above us from our igloo during our entire stay. It was nothing short of stupendous. It was a wonderful experience watching the Northern Lights in Franco's embrace every night. I was mesmerized.

During the day, we tried the restaurants in the area, checked out the shops, and walked in the forest. I was still feeling exhilarated after we returned from our trip. It was such a rewarding experience. That was one down from my bucket list.

* * *

Before I know it, Franco already checked out the hot-air balloons. He received some feedback that the best ride is from Cappadocia in Turkey. He was just as interested in riding on one and excited as I was because it was something he had not done himself. He had been to Cappadocia, but not on a hot-air balloon.

"I hope you don't have acrophobia or fear of heights," he commented.

"Fortunately, I have no such fear. This is something I've also been long wanting to try."

Franco favored the Private Flight with a maximum of four passengers on board, which included the two bodyguards. Carlo made our bookings online.

We took the flight to Turkey, and checked into a hotel. The balloon operator picked us up very early the next morning. After giving us the flight instructions, we were off. The balloon gradually accelerated into the air, just as a glorious sunrise surfaced on the horizon. It was a sight to behold. We hovered over the valleys and caves, including Cappadocia's fairy chimneys and astonishing landscapes. What a fantastic view from above. When we finally touched down after the two-hour flight, we were served breakfast and champagne on the ground.

Franco included visiting the graduated natural pools of Pamukkale in our itinerary since we were already in Turkey. Pamukkale is situated in the inner Aegean region. The natural graduated terrain of the pools somewhat resembles the way the Banawe rice terraces in the Philippines were built, but these ones are natural formations, and one can actually take a dip in them. The water was cool as we submerged ourselves in it, and we enjoyed the refreshing dip, including the bodyguards. It was something to experience. Those were two more down from my bucket list.

I intimated to Franco that we did not have to accomplish what are on my bucket list all at once. Fulfilling three of them already extremely satisfied me. There will be other times for more sights to see. I could not just take the King away from his responsibilities in the Kingdom, so they needed to be scheduled at the proper time.

Chapter

13

The patron saint of Marvella is St. Francis of Assisi. His Feast Day on October 4 is a holiday in the Kingdom. The people of Marvella bring their animals to the plaza to have them blessed by the priest. It was a coincidence that it was also my 61st birthday. I did not need a Queen's Day because the day itself is already a holiday. So, it was actually a fulfillment of my wish not to have my own day.

The day was marked by a colorful procession of people and their animals, some adorned attractively and some riding on decorated wagons, originating from the Cathedral of St. Francis and ending at the plaza. The royal family witnessed the festivities from the Palace balcony during mid-afternoon. There were all sorts of animals, and the grandkids enjoyed watching the blessing. The animals in the castle were not part of it because the priest already came over to bless them the day before. So, Khaleesi had her sprinkle of holy water earlier.

* * *

I had no inkling that Franco was up to something for my birthday. He earlier requested Chef Martin to present me with a big, square, and beautifully decorated cake with a spray of sugar flowers bearing the inscription "Happy Birthday! Queen Marianne". It was a delicious strawberry shortcake, which we all loved, especially the grandkids. Chef Martin also prepared dinner for the family which was fit for a Queen with roast turkey as the centerpiece. Then Franco grabbed my hand, and we walked to the library.

"Happy Birthday, darling," he greeted me, and handed me a small box.

"I thought no more gifts."

"For me, not for you."

I brought out the content of the box. It was a solid gold bracelet etched with two hearts inscribed with "Franco" and "Marianne". I hugged and kissed him.

"Thank you, love. This is so beautiful. I don't think I'd want to take this off too." The inscriptions on the gift sealed our love for each other. My husband also displayed his romantic side, but I already knew that side of his character.

I did not expect Franz and Tania to give me any presents for my birthday, but as they greeted me, they both handed me a gift – an embroidered shawl made in

Marvella from Tania and family, and a book and a set of lovely note pads from Franz and family. They both personally expressed to me their gratitude for loving their father.

"We've never seen Papa this happy before. It's wonderful seeing him like this. He loves you very much," Tania expressed to me.

"I love him deeply too," I responded.

"You're perfect for each other," Franz added. Getting the approval of Franco's children brought a smile to my face.

* * *

"Darling, do you notice that since we got married, we haven't quarreled or disagreed?" I posed the question to my King.

"You're right. You seem to always take my side. Am I being too controlling?"

"Not at all. Maybe I just happen to agree with your side, and I feel good when I do. That's a good sign, isn't it?"

"Yes, of course. I'm glad that we don't disagree, darling. We married late, so we should make every moment special every day of our life. I promise to make it my lifetime mission to please you."

"You're already doing that, and I don't know if I can be any happier than this. Can you imagine if we fight and fall out of love for each other? I shudder at the thought."

"I won't dwell on that thought. So far, you've made me the happiest man alive."

"I'm so glad to hear that. I still can't believe that I'd meet someone like you who would change my life forever."

* * *

I realized that any marriage could not be all that perfect, and that every relationship needed constant nurturing. This came to light with the visit of King Wilhelm of the constitutional Kingdom of Branthe. He arrived in Marvella to discuss with King Franco a reciprocal trade agreement. From the moment we were introduced, this visiting King in his early 60s of about my age gave me his undivided attention. He did not mask his admiration for me, and Franco noticed this. King Wilhelm happened to be an attractive monarch, a widower, and without a Queen. As part of the host Kingdom, I was obligated to be attentive towards him as our guest. During the social event we hosted at the castle in his honor, he asked only me to dance with him, and he did not ask anybody else. This did not escape Franco's observation. It was just a one-day visit, but it stirred a ripple in our marriage. After that uneventful visit, Franco appeared sullen.

"Darling, is there something wrong?" I inquired. "You seem to act differently towards me."

"No. Don't worry about it."

"It's just that I observe you're not your usual self, and you're not communicative towards me. Are you angry with me?"

"It's not anger. You were just doing your duty as Queen."

"What is it then?"

"I was overcome with jealousy. It hurt me seeing you dancing with King Wilhelm and smiling at him. I can't blame you for being beautiful, and he obviously admires you."

"I'm sorry if you were hurt, but it didn't mean anything to me. I was just being a good hostess to our guest." I was affected by Franco's reaction, and I could not hold back my tears.

He saw me like this, and immediately pulled me into his arms. "I don't want you to cry, and I never want to see you like this again. I'm sorry, love. I've never felt jealousy before. You're too precious to me."

"It pains me to see you hurt. I'll never hurt you. Please believe me. I will never be like other Queens who had illicit liaisons. How can I ever be unfaithful when I feel that I'm the luckiest woman on earth to be loved by you? You'll always be my one and only King."

I had no idea that jealousy could rear its ugly head without my intention. I was just trying to be a good Queen. I gave him a tight hug and I kissed him repeatedly to assure him of my words. I got my King back with that smile I love. From then on, when we had royal visitors, I limited my role in entertaining them, and left it to the others as much as possible.

* * *

It was Bianca's First Holy Communion. Franco is always present during special events in his family's life, which include his grandchildren. The ceremony was held at the Cathedral. We saw small boys and girls in identical white attire lining up to receive the host. Bianca was lovely in her dress – calf-length white dress and a veil with a pink ribbon at the waist for the girls, and a long-sleeved shirt and short pants for the boys with a light blue cravat. She waved and smiled at us when she spotted us inside the Cathedral. She was such a cute sight, and we waved and smiled back at her. Bianca is Tania's only child. She is quite close to her grandfather like the other grandkids, and she adores her father Justin.

The King's presence during certain occasions in the Kingdom, even in minor events, was appreciated by the people. They usually approach and greet him, and he always responds positively. He spent time talking to each of them after the First Communion rites. I was drawn into their conversations, and I joined in. One of the women in our book club had a son who was also a first communicant, and we chatted briefly. Franco always spares some time for the people. I have a lot to learn from him. I observed him when he was talking to them. He concentrates on the moment, and he listens intently to what they share. I love watching him speak and smile in his most lovable way. I can never stop loving this man.

We had breakfast in the castle. Chef Martin prepared pancakes, Bianca's favorite, and he produced a pink cake with a figure of a girl in white on top of it, and she squealed with delight. It was Bianca's day, and it made her very happy. I gave her a pearl rosary as our gift to her, and she thanked and hugged Franco and me.

Chapter

14

I urged the King to resume working on his book, especially now that he has an in-house Editor. He was amused with the reference to my role.

"Is the monarchy going to shoulder the expenses in the printing and distribution of your book, and do you intend to give everyone a copy?" I asked Franco.

"That's my plan. I want every Marvellan to read the book and own a copy. It's going to be about them and their home country. The monarchy will spend for it."

"It need not be every person. You can give a copy to every family, and they can share it with their family members."

"That's more like it. It can be part of the centerpiece of their home."

"In fact, the monarchy can even save money if we organize fund-raising endeavors to cover expenses."

"Have you thought of something?"

"I can set up a business. I haven't decided yet exactly what, but I'm thinking of something related to food. The proceeds of it can be funneled into the expenses for the book. I need to research further on it."

"Isn't that going to burden you, sweetheart? I don't want you working too hard."

"No, it's not going to be a burden. Give me a little time to look into it."

"Okay then. I'll leave it up to you. You have so many ideas stored up in that pretty little head of yours."

* * *

When I decided to visit the green garden, I instantly had a light-bulb moment. Why not produce pickled vegetables? It is called *achara* in Filipino. The Korean version is called *kimchi*. I could actually combine both recipes. I got fired up with the idea that I immediately checked on the various recipes found on the internet.

The following day, Franco left for the Palace, and while he was gone, I gathered the ingredients I needed from the castle's vegetable patch with Sergio's help, and brought them to the royal kitchen. I advised Ms. Ethel and the kitchen staff that I was going to test something, and I did not need any help. They left me alone. Initially, I was not exactly pleased with the immediate result. The second attempt was slightly better. I add a little more spice, and it came out perfect to my taste.

The royal kitchen happened to have a stock of mason jars for use in preserves. I asked them for two boxes with a dozen jars each. When I had filled up the jars, I designed the proper labels on the computer, printed them out, and attached them to the bottles. I identified them as "Pickled Vegetables" with the brand name "Marvelous". Then one of the kitchen staff transported them to the weekend market to sell after putting a reasonable price tag on them. When she returned at the end of the day, she reported that they were all sold out, and some people were looking for more. That was my go-signal.

I was excited to tell Franco about my initial success. The next step was to go on a bigger scale. I already had a steady supply of vegetables from the royal garden, plus the garden club would have the ready market for their produce. When Franco learned of the favorable outcome of my business venture, he offered me the barn within the castle grounds which was not in use. He suggested I set up my business paraphernalia there with the help of the carpenters. I was excited over the prospect. I ordered a stove, more mason jars, and the tools for preparing the vegetables. When the carpenters were done with building the shelves and providing the work tables, I borrowed two of the kitchen staff to help me prepare and bottle the pickles.

We were able to produce initially 300 bottles of pickles a week. Again, they were all sold out at the weekend market. I decided to increase production. It meant hiring workers from outside. I was able to hire five workers the following week, and I paid them on a weekly basis. News of our pickled vegetables spread among those who frequent the weekend market. Consumers learned to serve them as appetizer. It was something new and agreeable to their taste.

I had no big plans of growing the business any bigger because it would entail hiring more people, and I could supervise only a small number. I wanted it to be a hands-on business for me. Besides, I was relying mainly on the produce of the green garden. I pegged my production at 1,000 bottles a week. It continued to sell like hotcakes at the weekend market. A restaurant also had a standing weekly order, and they picked up the boxed bottles from us. It raked in the needed initial funds for the book. I gave Chef Martin a few bottles of it to sample. He served it to us during one of our meals, and Franco liked it.

"How ingenious of you to label your vegetable pickles 'Marvelous'. I like it." Franco credited me with his feedback.

"It just came to mind. Now we have the seed money for your book. It's a start."

"I have you to thank for. As I've said before, you never cease to amaze me, my darling."

Chapter

15

As my pickle business succeeded and continued to earn, I toyed with another fund-raising project for the book which could be a one-time effort. I was immediately prompted to put up an art exhibit. Since Franco and I both paint, we can display and sell our artworks at the museum. I figured it would draw a good crowd, considering they are done by royalty. I was not too sure about my own drawing power, but I was absolutely certain that people would want to buy and own a painting by the King. I broached my idea to him.

"An art exhibit of our works? Are you sure about this?" He sounded skeptical.

"Why not? Many people would want to have your paintings. You have many admirers, love. I'm not sure about mine, but I can go for the ride. Who knows?"

"Come to think of it, it does sound like a good idea. Where are these ideas coming from? You astound me, sweetheart," he responded with a pleased expression.

"I know people will not hesitate to buy the paintings, especially when they learn that the proceeds will go into the publication of your book. It's for a good cause for the citizens of Marvella."

* * *

I believed that maybe we could each do 25 paintings, or a total of 50 paintings. We work on different subjects, so there will be variety. I paint landscapes, flowers, and still life. While Franco can do these too, he paints animals, including horses, and humans. We can always hold another exhibit if the paintings get sold out. It will definitely raise money for the book.

Franco ordered canvases of various sizes for us to work on. He earlier provided me with a new easel. The castle has an adjunct room in the library which is some sort of a large-enough separate office, and he converted it into our studio. I used to paint with oil, but when I discovered acrylic, I prefer it now because it dries up fast. I brought my acrylic paints with me when I moved to Marvella. I was looking forward to the painting sessions with my husband.

I computed that it would take us each a month to finish 25 paintings. I was able to finish a painting in one day, depending on its size. We agreed not to work on large canvases because they would take a longer time. So, we chose the regular-size canvases, not too big nor too small. We painted our subject vertically or horizontally. We planned to exhibit them framed in identical simple brown borders, and the buyers will have the liberty to change them if they have preferred frames.

I got us two aprons from the kitchen to protect our clothes when we painted. We started after breakfast one morning when Franco did not have to go to the Palace. We spent practically the whole day holed up in the studio. A palace staff served us lunch and snacks. The studio has comfortable chairs, in case we want to take a rest.

Towards afternoon, Franco was half-done with his painting of roaming horses, and I was almost finished with my vase of flowers from Pinterest.

"I feel like having ice cream," he announced. "Do you want some?"

"Yes. I won't refuse ice cream."

"Let's ask for sundae." He called the kitchen on the intercom and requested them to bring us low-fat ice cream sundae without the whipping cream. In a few minutes, we were enjoying our sundae during a break from painting. I loved these moments with my husband. It is the togetherness which I value greatly.

* * *

We had our usual dinner with the family. Franco always asked the grandkids about their day and followed up on the progress in their studies. He listened to each of them and asked them questions. He often joked with them, and they reacted with amusement and glee. He talked to them in Italian and English, and I enjoyed listening to their conversations.

After dinner, Franco and I had decaf coffee in the receiving area, and we were joined by Franco and Tania with their spouses, Ara and Justin. Ara is from Marvella and Justin is French. Ara is a musician and handles music classes for kids. Justin is a professor and teaches at the university. The grandkids all play a musical instrument. Ara sat at the piano and proceeded to play a classical piece by Chopin. Afterwards, I requested her to play Debussy's "Claire de Lune", which is one of my favorites, and she played it beautifully.

The grandkids had ice cream in the royal kitchen later on. Franco encourages them to interact occasionally with the castle staff. It is part of their social connection because Franco wants them to appreciate all types of people. That is how he raised Franz and Tania, and he was now passing on the same values to his grandchildren.

Chapter

16

"Darling, now that the castle is your home, feel free to make changes or buy anything you want," the King suggested.

"There's nothing that needs changing. It's perfect as it is. Who did the interiors? I like the way it's executed."

"We hired an interior decorator, and he did a very good job."

"By the way, is Chef Martin a full-time chef in the castle?"

"Practically, but he's here mostly during daytime, and he sometimes delegates some of the cooking to the kitchen staff with his strict instructions. He is aware of my food choices, and he sticks to healthy ingredients. He has his own restaurant where he spends time in the evenings. It's named after him. I'll take you there sometime."

"I'd like that. I love his cooking."

* * *

The King and I did not exactly have a date time like regular couples, who eat out on a particular day in a week, because he could not just show up in any restaurant. He confessed that he felt guilty about this, but I assured him that it was really not that important to me as long as we had our meals together.

"I'll make up for it, love. I'll find a way," he promised, taking my hand in his.

"Don't worry about it. I'm perfectly fine with it. I know that a King can't just make a public appearance any time."

"We can still go outside of Marvella. I'm thinking, why don't we have dinner at Chef Martin's restaurant tomorrow? Maybe he can give us a private room, so we won't be too conspicuous."

"Wow, I'd love that."

The next morning, Franco talked to Chef Martin about his dinner plan, and the latter said he could get us in by the back entrance so we would not be noticed. He was enthusiastic to reserve a private room for us. We arrived at the restaurant before 7:00 p.m., and Chef Martin met us and whisked us to our private table.

"Chef, we're not on a strict diet today, so you can serve us your specialties," Franco disclosed. "Remember, we are paying customers, so no *pro bono* because this is your business." Chef Martin smiled at the King's statement. He himself served us our meal with a choice of white or red wine. We feasted on his culinary concoctions of chicken, prawns, salmon, and a pasta-broccoli dish with complicated foreign labels I could not recall. The cuisine was predominantly Italian. Our meal was simply superb, and the ice cream dessert was out of this world.

"You're an amazing chef," I complimented Chef Martin. "That was a most delicious meal."

"Thank you, Your Majesty. I value your compliment," he replied.

"I need to exercise more after this indulgence," Franco expressed. "So, Chef, we're back to our normal Mediterranean menu tomorrow." Chef Martin laughed.

Chef Martin serves us not-so-healthy foods occasionally, like fried chicken and hamburgers. It is okay with Franco if it is not often, and for the sake of the grandkids, who love such foods. Franco and I both crave for all-in burgers once in a while. It is barbecue night once a week at the castle *al fresco*. Chef Martin's culinary expertise is not limited to Mediterranean cuisine, and he is innovative too.

From then on, Franco made it a point that we have a date night at least once a month. We usually go out of Marvella where nobody can recognize us. He is that thoughtful of a husband. We relish these times immensely where we have a private conversation during dinner and simply enjoy each other's company.

* * *

After dinner one night, we proceeded to the receiving area, and the parents allowed the grandkids to join us before their scheduled bedtime. The discussion focused on the forthcoming enrolment of Francesco at Eton. It was Francesco's first time to be away from home, and both Franco and Franz assured him that it is going to be fun, and regaled him with stories of their schooldays, which somehow put to rest any of his fears. Francesco is a very good-looking boy with Franco's and Franz' dominant features. He is third in succession. The topic changed course when the girls joined in.

"*Nonno*, you love *Nonna* very much, don't you?", Bianca asked unexpectedly.

"Yes, of course. Why do you ask, Bianca?"

"Because you're always kissing her." The girls went into a fit of giggles. We all laughed too.

"When you love someone dearly, you kiss and hug them often," Franco enlightened her.

"I want that too when I grow up," Olivia expressed.

"Me too, *Nonno*," Bianca countered.

"Come here, you two." The girls rushed to Franco's side, and he hugged and kissed them. He brought them over to me, and I hugged and kissed them too. I have learned to love his grandkids like they are my own.

Chapter

17

Town Hall meetings are held at least quarterly to discuss and settle certain issues in the Kingdom. It serves as a forum to gather the sentiments of the people on pressing concerns. The Palace venue is the Throne Room since the ultimate decisions on all issues rest on the King. Attendance is on a first come-first served basis to ensure that everybody has a seat to its full capacity. The 12 members of the Royal Court regulate the meetings, but Franco always makes his presence visible. The King imposes the final judgment since they are an absolute monarchy. One such meeting came around unexpectedly due to its urgency, and Franco expressed that I should attend it with him because I am now Queen. We arrived at the Palace in the morning at the start of working hours, and we occupied our places at the ubiquitous elevated thrones on top of the steps.

The Royal Court members sat at the long table right below the steps, facing the audience.

The mood of the meeting was dismal, owing to the nature of the principal issue. A young girl was brutally raped and she succumbed to her wounds after a week in the hospital. The 40-year-old rapist was identified and caught. It was the first such case in the Kingdom, so it caused a furor among the people. Half of the people were in favor of hanging the criminal as payment for his heinous crime. A heated discussion ensued, and conflicting views were bared between the two clashing groups. Mavellans are allowed to express their opinions during Town Hall meetings. The King steps in when it is decision time. My admiration for my husband grew more at this instance.

The King addresses the audience:

"My dear people of Marvella, we are a Catholic Kingdom and we do not sanction the death penalty in any form. This is how we were brought up in our Catholic faith. We have no right to take a life because only God can do that. I know that this criminal deserves to be punished for what he did to this innocent girl, and this angers all of us. If we hang him, we are playing God, and that would be wrong. God has the sole right to judge all men, and we will be taking that away from Him. If you feel a strong disgust for this criminal, banish that feeling and leave it in God's Hands. I support the verdict of putting this criminal in prison for many years, and the seclusion will be a severe enough punishment for his crime."

I witnessed for myself that in Marvella, the King has the last word. The people accepted the King's judgment, and the criminal was sentenced to 70 years in prison without parole. The family of the victim believed the sentence was fair and it accorded them sufficient vindication. Franco and I approached the family of the victim afterwards to express our sympathy.

"I'm impressed with your decision," I mentioned to Franco after leaving the Palace.

"It's the only way to go. People forget that we have to abide by our faith. We can't play God," he emphasized.

I am beginning to comprehend Franco's supreme authority as King of Marvella. He has absolute power over the government, and his authority is not restricted to any written laws. He is tasked with administrative powers, the imposition of taxes, justice, and foreign policy, with the support of the Royal Court. The number of absolute monarchies in the world is declining, and Marvella remains one of them. The Vatican itself is considered an absolute monarchy. The people of Marvella seem content in their Kingdom. Some of the compelling reasons are because their taxes are low, the incidence of crime is practically zero, and their citizens live comfortably.

I am forever grateful that I married a Catholic King. We espouse the same Christian values and observe the feasts of the Church. A priest comes regularly to celebrate Mass at the castle chapel, and we attend Church services together.

* * *

We received disturbing news from Carlo that a busload of employees from the dairy factory crashed into a tree a day before on their way home from work. He said that the report which reached him attributed the accident to a bursting tire. The driver could not control the vehicle and deliberately rammed it into a tree to avoid the ravine. It carried 55 passengers, with 20 suffering from serious injuries and immediately brought to the hospital. One of the passengers, a man who was seated in the front row, was in critical condition and in a coma. Some of the passengers had only minor cuts and were out-patients.

The King was saddened by this news. I accompanied him to look into the victims at the hospital. We stopped at each of the victim's bed to talk and offer comforting words. There were 12 men and 8 women with serious injuries. They were all glad to have their King visit them at the hospital. The man in a coma was in a separate room, and the doctors were monitoring his condition. As we entered his room, the doctors and nurses all bowed. Franco approached his bed and held his hand. He spoke softly to the man, assuring him of prayers and help even if the man was not conscious. He asked the doctors about the man's chances of waking up. The lead doctor answered that they still need to observe him for a few days, but his vital signs were strong, and that was encouraging. The man's head was wrapped in a bandage because of a minor concussion.

In the next days, Franco continued to follow up on the victims' individual progress. We visited the hospital a second time and talked to the patients. Only a few of them with less serious injuries were released after two weeks, but the man in a coma remained unresponsive. On the third week when we paid a succeeding visit, we were met by one of the doctors with the good news that the man in a coma was now awake. Franco was glad to see him awake. He talked to him at length, and assured him that he would be all right. I could read in the man's face that he appreciated his King's visit and concern.

Chapter

18

"By the way, darling, I forgot to mention to you that as Queen, you are entitled to a yearly allowance. It's not as much as that of the Queen of England, but it's a substantial amount," Franco revealed to me.

"Really? But I don't need it. I have an idea. Why don't I donate the amount to the printing of your book?"

"No, I won't allow you to do that. That's your money and I want you to spend it on yourself."

"I don't need anything, love."

"I want you to keep it. When we travel, you'll want to buy some things, so you'll find some need for it. You'll think of something, darling."

"Who do I thank for it?"

"Nobody. It's from the monarchy."

* * *

After several months in Marvella, I still had not explored the length, width, and breadth of the Kingdom. I learned that, aside from the plaza's open space, they have a People's Hall, where large activities are held, a spacious theater for cultural shows, a huge gymnasium for sports events with an Olympic-size indoor pool, and a polo field. It is a separate island Kingdom, so it also has endless stretches of sand and seashore with pristine beaches.

Franco is an avid polo player. In his restored physical condition, he resumed playing polo with renewed enthusiasm. I watched him in one of their games with visiting players from a nearby country. I love horses, so it is a pleasure to watch their games. Franco is an excellent polo player, and he easily took the lead to victory for his team. He expertly maneuvered his black horse, Thunder, on the field. I was so proud of him. He was smiling after his team's victory, and I congratulated him. I was ready with a towel to mop his face of sweat. I like seeing him happy like this.

* * *

When I think of the children of Marvella, I feel prodded to organize a regular activity for them. *Why not have a Children's Day?*, I said to myself. It is something the children can look forward to. It can be a monthly event at the People's Hall. I divulged my plans to Lola, and she immediately devised a program for such a day. Franco had no objections, even after my telling him that

I intended to use my personal funds from my Queen's allowance.

It covered a week of planning the event. We scheduled the day on a Saturday morning with games, a clown, a magician, and ending with lunch. Lola gathered volunteers to help us in preparing the prizes and loot bags for the children, and supervising the games. Our main assistants were Francesco, Olivia, and Bianca. It was a good opportunity for the children of Marvella to rub elbows with the royal children.

It is always a rewarding experience seeing the smiles on children's faces. Franco made his appearance during lunch, and the children were all excited to meet their King. For lunch, we served burgers, sausages, pasta, ice cream, and juice, and Franco ate with them. The royal kids were happy to see their *Nonno* also join in the conversations with the children. I listened in to the questions the children asked him, and he answered them to the children's satisfaction.

One 10-year-old boy boldly suggested the revival of the sport of jousting, which kings of old used to sponsor. He justified that Marvella is a Kingdom, and jousting is a sport of kings.

"That's out of the question, young man. Jousting is an old sport with the goal of killing the other party. It has long been abolished. Marvella does not favor violence. We are a peaceful modern-day kingdom, so we should promote safe sports," the King explained. "Do you play any sport?"

"Yes, Your Majesty. I play rugby in school."

"That's a great sport. I used to play rugby myself. Practice your game and try to play well."

"Your Majesty, can the Kingdom sponsor movies for the family?" a small girl inquired.

"Certainly. I'll make arrangements for that. We can show movies at the theater. We just need to be strict with classification. No children during adult movies." The children laughed in unison.

A small boy of about five had a question: "Your Majesty, do you have a sword?"

"Yes, I own one. However, I do not use it. It's on display at the castle. We do not fight with swords anymore, young man."

Then the same small boy followed it up with another question. "Your Majesty, when do you wear your crown?"

"Only on special and important events. Thank God, because it's heavy." The children laughed again, finding the King's comment funny. "I hope I answered your questions, children. I cannot promise to be present with you every month, but I'll try my best to join you when I'm free." The children applauded their King, and they all stood and bowed as he exited the Hall.

He is not only the people's King, but also the children's King. The children had a wonderful time and looked forward to the next Children's Day.

* * *

Marvella has a growing population of elderly people. My next target was the seniors. The Kingdom has a hospice for the elderly where they can stay for proper care when they are no longer ambulatory or functional. My program was a weekly hospice visit to check on the well-being of the elderly and to bring them cheer. Most of them are lonely, so our visit is always highly anticipated. We visited the elderly bearing gifts, usually food, and things they could use. We also played music so they could sing or dance along. We sang and danced with them, and it became a lively affair. The hospice has a team of caregivers, and the patients are getting adequate care. One can grow old comfortably in Marvella without fear of being forgotten or abandoned.

Chapter

19

It actually took Franco and me almost two months to finish our paintings because he was free only on certain days. I worked faster than he did because I was home most of the time. We finally finished all our paintings, and Carlo scheduled an art exhibit. He arranged to have it advertised and known even beyond Marvella's borders. The art exhibit was launched during cocktails held at the museum. It was advertised as a fund-raising event for the book. I could not believe the size of the crowd it attracted.

Luminaries from other countries were our guests, and Franco introduced me to them. I got to meet other royals and prominent personages. We mingled with the large crowd and moved around the museum floor, absorbing comments here and there about our paintings. Most of them could not believe that we are indeed artists, and are capable of producing such artworks.

We can call our common style as more contemporary, and not modern, because we paint our subject as is. We signed our artworks simply as "Franco V" and "Marianne I". A prince from a neighboring Kingdom purchased 10 of our paintings. Towards the night, all paintings had the sign "Sold" on them. Franco and I were overly pleased with the turnout.

A royal cousin of Franco, who is a Duke, advised him to produce more paintings because he divulged that there were some who still wanted to buy them. This prompted Franco and me to mull over this. His cousin pointed out that the suggestion originated from some Marvellans who were not able to buy any painting.

"What do you think of the suggestion?", Franco asked me.

"I can do more paintings, but how about you? Do you have the time, love?"

"I can manage a few more. This will be of a smaller scale since it will purely be for Marvellans."

* * *

We were back in the studio painting. While I was busy painting, I happened to glance towards Franco's direction, and I caught him looking at me.

"What? Why are you looking at me like that?" He had that same look with the slightly lowered head and eyes fixed on me. My husband likes to tease me.

"I'm just admiring my wife. You're very beautiful."

"Franco, don't make me blush again," I begged him.

He smiled, approached me, and pulled me gently from my seat. "Come, let's take a rest from painting and enjoy each other. The door of the studio is locked, so we have all the privacy. Darling, I just can't get enough of you."

Golly, how can I not love this man, who is full of surprises, and provides me with limitless excitement?

* * *

Carlo arranged a second art exhibit at the museum after Franco and I finished 25 paintings. This time it was not advertised and was known only within the Kingdom. The cocktail hour was attended by a sizeable crowd of Marvellans. Franco and I discussed art with them and answered their questions. At the end of the day, our paintings were all sold out. I could not imagine something like this happening to me. I considered myself merely as an amateurish painter. Franco is a better painter than I am.

Chapter

20

Jesse's daughter Mia, who is also my godchild, communicated with me on Face Time to tell me about her forthcoming marriage. She wanted Franco and me to be her principal sponsors at her wedding. Her groom was her American boss in her place of work who was ten years her senior. I was happy for her. It meant that we needed to go to the Philippines for the wedding. I discussed this with Franco, and he was quick to agree to the trip.

"This must be the first time that a King and a Queen will be principal sponsors at a wedding. I'll be doing this for Mia. Maybe there won't be any publicity since we're already married. I just hope so," I imparted to Franco.

"I understand. We can keep our movements insignificant, like what I used to do *incognito*. Just think that we'll be going back to the place where we first met."

"That's the only significance to me. Of course, I'm excited to see family and friends. Since we'll already be in the Philippines, I want to take you at least to my hometown Cebu, and maybe to nearby Bohol to see the sights."

"I look forward to that, darling. I want to see your roots and the rest of your country of birth."

We discussed our itinerary with Carlo, who did all the bookings for us. Franco also wanted him to be with us during the trip plus the two bodyguards. Carlo scheduled two weeks for the entire trip, and I thought to myself that it seemed long, but I did not express this to Franco. The wedding came first, and after that, the southern trips, but I envisioned them to be just short visits. I decided to wear my own wedding dress so my relatives could actually see it. The *jusi* material has just the right color for a wedding sponsor's gown, and it is classy and elegant. I try to refrain from spending much on myself, except when it is absolutely necessary. I have never been an extravagant person.

Mia's wedding was a month away, so we had ample time to prepare for our trip. Franco had to make arrangements in the Palace in his absence. This must be the longest time that he would be gone from the Kingdom. He has a reliable working Royal Court, and Franz already acts as his deputy, being his direct successor.

I delegated my work to Lola, who was familiar with our projects. I drew up a list of to-dos for her to follow, and I could rely on her.

PART 3

Blessings

Chapter

1

We boarded the royal jet and arrived in Manila a day before the wedding. Carlo booked us all earlier at Raffles Hotel.

The wedding on a Saturday was at historic Manila Cathedral, which I was eager for Franco to see. The reception was at the Manila Hotel. The wedding was solemnized during late afternoon. Mia was one enchanting bride as she walked down the aisle in Jesse's arm. Franco wore a suit and tie like the other male principal sponsors, and he still stood out. His navy blue suit matched the color of his eyes, and his tie had a paisley design. This was my first time to see him dressed like this, and he looked splendid and handsome as ever. We took the lead among the principal sponsors. The guests wanted to catch a glimpse of a real King and Queen, so we became the center of attention, especially when we were announced as King Franco V and Queen

Marianne I of Marvella. It was Franco's idea to give Mia and her groom an Asian cruise for their honeymoon as our wedding gift.

The reception was a lively affair, and Franco met my relatives. His presence briefly stole the spotlight from the newlyweds. I could see that he was enjoying himself too. The festivity continued well into the late hours, and we danced the night away with gusto. It was the first time for my relatives to interact with Franco, so this was indeed a worthwhile visit. They were all fascinated to learn that we now have a King and a Queen in our family. They were all amused when Franco uttered "*Hala ka*" like a native. My King fitted in with my family, and that was a blessing. Fortunately, our presence in the country was mentioned only by two newspaper columnists, without any photos of us, so our privacy was not sacrificed. It was perhaps because Marvella is a Kingdom not known to many. However, a photo of us taken in Church appeared in a magazine and was labeled simply as "The King and Queen of Marvella," with no additional details. I heaved a sigh of relief.

The following day was a Sunday. Jesse treated us to a day trip to Tagaytay so Franco could view Taal Volcano. We all rode in a van with Christine and Rafael, and had lunch at Taal Vista Lodge, which offered tourists a cultural show. Franco was intrigued to know that Taal is a volcano within a volcano. He appreciated Filipino food, and I let him try some of the local delicacies. I am glad he has an adventurous palate.

On our way back from Tagaytay, I asked Jesse to make a brief stop at the Legaspi park. I wanted us to revisit the spot where Franco and I first laid eyes on each other.

"Familiar?", I asked Franco as we alighted at the park entrance.

"Of course. It's the scene of the crime," he joked. "This is where I first met her and I fell in love instantly," he declared to our party. "The bodyguards were our witnesses. I was seated on this bench, and her dog Khaleesi dragged her to me. Smart dog." Franco then reached for my hand as the memory of that fateful day descended upon us.

* * *

Mia did not need my condo anymore after her marriage since her new husband had a bigger one, so I allowed Rafael to occupy it. It is an asset which can remain in the family for as long as someone in the family has a need for it. Earlier, I took out some of the things I left behind to bring to Marvella.

While in the Philippines, I knew I should do some shopping for clothes and items to bring home to Franco's family and the castle staff because prices here are reasonable, and there is a wider range of choices. From the hotel, I planned to go to Landmark and Rustan's by myself, but Franco insisted that I am accompanied by one of the bodyguards. I followed his order, and my obedience paid off because I had someone to carry my purchases.

* * *

Sofia organized a lunch with our classmates. She picked a function room which could accommodate all 20 of us. It had to be a private function room because women can generate a lot of noise when they are together. This group recently discovered that I married a King when Sofia finally revealed it to them, and everyone was eager to hear my story. I brought items from Marvella for all my classmates. Their questions came one after the other.

"So, Marianne, you now have the title of Queen? That's amazing." Paula said.

"Yes. I didn't want it in the beginning, but my husband won't hear of it. I'm still not used to being addressed as 'Your Majesty', and when people stand and bow before us."

They were anxious to know how Franco looks like. I said that to me he is the handsomest man I have ever met, and he is actually my story-book Prince Charming.

"He has a great physique. His abs are even flatter than mine. He's health-conscious, which I appreciate so I can stay healthy too. The castle has an in-house chef who prepares and supervises our food. See my husband for yourself. He's coming to pick me up later, and I'll introduce him to all of you."

"What's he like as a husband?", Ana inquired.

"He's the perfect husband, caring, and very *cariñoso* (loving). He tells me 'I love you' many times a day, sometimes in Italian, which I'm learning to speak. He kisses and hugs me all the time, and I love it."

"How romantic. You're so lucky, Marianne," Lissa commented.

"Is Italian the language of Marvella?" Ana followed up.

"Yes, plus British English. Franco happens to speak five languages."

"Wow, how impressive. How good a king is he, and what sets him apart from other men?" Alicia questioned.

"Franco is a dynamic King, and the people of Marvella love him. When he appears in public, people flock to him because he speaks and listens to them. He's not condescending, considering his stature, and he treats people as equal. He can be controlling too, which I like. Besides, he's King, so it's all right. I never dreamt that I'd meet someone like him. You know me. I planned to remain single all my life, but he made me fall in love with him."

My classmates were impressed with my glowing description of Franco. Sofia also added her positive opinion of him. When Franco appeared, I stood to greet him. They were all agog and excited to meet him. He was wearing a *barong tagalog* (Filipino men's wear), which I ordered for him earlier, and he looked distinguished in it. He kissed and hugged me in front of everybody, which confirmed what I shared with them earlier, and continued to wrap his arms around me. "I miss you", he said to me within their hearing.

"Classmates, let me introduce to you my beloved husband. I won't mention all your names anymore because they are too many for him to remember anyway," I explained.

"Hello, lovely ladies. I can see that this country has an abundance of beauty. I'm pleased to meet my wife's classmates," Franco declared with his captivating smile.

"*Ang guapo!* Marianne" (So handsome, Marianne), Lissa gushed. "*Sobra ka* sweet *pati*" (He's also extremely sweet).

"*Ang ganda din ng* accent" (He also has a beautiful accent.), Alicia countered.

"*Mukhang ang lakas pa at ang ganda ng katawan*" (He still looks strong and has a great body), Donna observed.

"I won't translate anymore, love," I explained to Franco. "They're all very positive comments about you." Everybody laughed, including Franco.

"Now, ladies, you can understand why Marianne gave up her being single," Sofia said, and they all nodded in agreement with plain admiration for Franco.

"If any of you happens to visit Europe, you're always welcome in Marvella as our guests. We'd love having you there," Franco extended the invitation to the group.

"Come and visit us anytime," I seconded Franco's invitation.

Chapter

2

Carlo booked us at the Marriott Hotel in Cebu. The hotel provided us with a van to take us around the city. We stayed for a day just to experience the city of my birth. We passed by our old house, which we had sold earlier when our parents passed away, to show Franco where I grew up. The big house still looked nice and had since then been repainted and refurbished. He was impressed with Cebu's progressive character. I said that it is a metropolitan city in the south next to Manila.

I brought all five of us to SM for them to try Cebu's specialty, the *lechon* (roasted pig). Franco liked it very much, but I cautioned him not to eat too much of it because it is not exactly healthy food. Carlo and the bodyguards obviously enjoyed eating it, and gave it their thumbs-up. I also let them try the fresh *mangoes*, which they all appreciated. I shared with Franco my plan of putting up a *mango* orchard in Marvella.

"Now I want to eat my favorite fruit. I miss it," I told Franco.

"What's your favorite fruit? It's not *mango*?". He wanted to know.

"It's *durian*. It must be the most controversial fruit. It's either you love it or you hate it. It's a spiny fruit which emits a pungent smell, but it's okay to those who love the fruit. It's a common delicacy to those from the south, like me, but most of the people from the north, except a few, shun it. It's a popular fruit especially in Singapore and Malaysia."

We found a fruit stall which sold *durian*, and it happened to have the *Mao Shang Wan* variety, which is one of the best. The vendor picked a perfectly shaped *durian* and broke it open. I did not want to force Franco to try it, but he did anyway. I watched his expression as he tasted the fruit flesh which covered the seed.

"I like it. It's rich. I didn't know there's such a fruit," he declared, and I sighed in relief that he liked it. Carlo also tried it and he liked it too, but the two bodyguards were not even remotely interested, and shook their heads when offered to try it.

* * *

The next morning, we joined the Bohol tour where we were picked up at our hotel to ride the ferry, which cruised Bohol Island, taking in the scenic countryside. Then we boarded the Loboc River Cruise, which is a slow-moving boat with Filipino food on board, and

Franco tasted more local food, which agreed with his palate. The next stop was Carmen to view the famous Chocolate Hills, and we marveled at the formation of successive natural mounds. We returned to Cebu by ferry where the royal jet awaited us.

On the royal jet where we were seated side by side, Franco kissed me on the cheek and whispered into my ear, "*Gihigugma ko ikaw*", which utterly surprised me.

"What did you just say?" I reacted with a jolt. He repeated the sentence in Cebuano, and I laughed.

"Where did you learn that?" I was curious to find out.

"I asked the hotel receptionist to teach me."

"Do you know what it means?"

"Of course. It means 'I love you', he affirmed with a naughty expression.

"You're very resourceful, love."

My husband learned one more language to express his love for me. How can I not feel happy?

* * *

Franco did not reveal to me until the last minute that we were proceeding to Dubai to see the Burg Khalifa, which was in my bucket list. He relished watching my reactions to his surprises. I learned later that Carlo booked us in a hotel for an overnight stay. Burg Khalifa is one of the tallest buildings in the world. We were able to go up to the top, where we actually saw the curvature of the Earth due to its sheer height. I was simply awed. One more down from my bucket list. I was not expecting Franco to tell me that there was still one more destination in our itinerary.

"I thought this is the end of our trip. Where are we headed?" I questioned him.

"One more place to visit – the Taj Mahal."

I literally jumped off my seat. "Are you serious?"

"Never more serious, sweetheart. I want you to be happy, so we're on our way there."

"Thank you, darling. You make me very happy again. It's getting to be a habit with you."

"I'll claim my reward later," he replied, teasing me again.

The majestic Taj Mahal is in Agra, India. It was built by the Emperor as a tomb for his favorite wife. That gave me the impression that he had other wives. The beautiful structure was built using ivory-white marble. It took more than 20 years to build. You can already admire this architectural wonder from afar until you reach the site itself. This was one more down, the fifth, from my bucket list.

"Tell me, love, is there anything else on your bucket list?, Franco asked me.

"The thing with a bucket list is that it continues to fill up. Oh, yes. I'd like to watch the Wimbledon matches."

"Okay, we'll schedule that. I play and like watching tennis myself, so that's something we can both enjoy."

* * *

We reserved a couple of days to rest our travel-weary bodies upon our return to the Kingdom. We had adequate night sleep and *siesta* to make sure we recovered from the effects of the common hassles of travel. On the third day of our arrival, the King went back to work and left for the Palace. I distributed the items I purchased in the Philippines to the castle staff, Mira and Chef Martin, and they appreciated my gesture. I also had things for Lola and her helpers in our various projects. I included the women who worked in our pickle business, Sergio the royal gardener, and the crafts supervisors.

Franco returned home from work mid-afternoon and drifted into a brief *siesta*. I served him decaf coffee as he woke up.

"How do you feel, darling? Did you get enough rest?" I asked him, running my fingers through his sexily tousled hair.

"I guess so because I feel invigorated. How about you?"

"I feel just fine. Do you want us to start working on your book? What do you think?"

"Why not? It's funny that this book project was what brought us together, and it's the first thing we shelved."

"How right you are. So much has happened during the year - our marriage, my move here and becoming Queen, your accident, our many trips, and various projects and events in the Kingdom which relegated the book to the backseat of our priorities. You're halfway through it, so let's work together to see this in print. This is your project."

"I agree. We met because of this book project. I can see its significance, even divine intervention. We were destined to meet and be together. Let's do this for Marbella."

Chapter

3

"Darling, I noticed that the music you constantly play are those of Frank Sinatra, Perry Como, Michael Buble, Julio Iglesias, and Il Divo. Are these your favorite artists?" Franco asked me, while looking through my collection.

"Oh, yes. Does the music I play bother you?"

"Of course not. These are great artists, and I appreciate their music too. Have you watched any of their concerts?"

"Only Michael Buble with Sofia back home, and we really enjoyed his concert. I'm a fan."

"We can actually invite them to perform in Marvella. Do you know that? With the exception of Frank Sinatra and Perry Como because they're already dead. The last one we had here were Tony Bennett for the more mature audience and One Direction for the young people, and both shows were successful. I want many Marvellans to get to witness such events, so the monarchy subsidizes part of the ticket cost."

"That's wonderful. You're such a good King. You're always concerned about the people."

* * *

The next thing Franco divulged to me was that Julio Iglesias and Il Divo were scheduled to perform in Marvella, and I was thrilled. We attended the separate concerts one after the other. The theater has a special balcony reserved for the King and Queen. We also got to meet the artists as a royal privilege. It is one advantage of being Queen. Julio Iglesias may have aged a bit, but he still exhibited a certain sex appeal. It was a pleasure meeting him, and his apparent charisma was admirable. He and Franco conversed in Spanish. The Il Divo members are great performers. They all sing well as a quartet and in their solos, and they are so good-looking in person, especially my favorite Sebastien.

* * *

"Darling, I want to do something for the castle staff," I suggested to the King.

"What do you have in mind?"

"How about honoring them at a party in the castle for their services? They all serve us well and I want us to show them our appreciation. Will you allow me to do something like that?"

"You don't need to ask my permission, my love. You're forgetting you're Queen, and you can make your own decisions."

"I have money from my allowance, and I intend to use it. Do they sell pigs at the Country Fair?"

"Pigs? What will you do with pigs? Are you planning to raise them?"

"No. I'm thinking of roasting them for the party in the castle. You liked the *lechon* you tasted in Cebu, didn't you?

"Yes. It was delicious."

"I want your family and the castle staff to try it. I'll guide Chef Martin in roasting them."

"I see. There's a Country Fair this weekend, and farmers come to sell their livestock and farm animals. I can take you there."

* * *

The visit by the King and Queen of Marvella at the Country Fair was unexpected by the people. There were various items on sale, and visitors from other countries always put this important event on their calendar. I was interested only in the pigs, so we proceeded to the area where they were displayed. Chef Martin came along with two of his kitchen staff in a separate vehicle that could hold and transport the pigs. He inspected the pigs and picked four of the medium-size ones. He was more knowledgeable in choosing the ones with the right fat ratio, and his men loaded them into the vehicle. The farmer, who owned the pigs, did not want to accept payment when he discovered that the buyers were the King and Queen, and he wanted to give them as gifts, but Franco refused. He even instructed Chef Martin to pay the farmer more than what they were worth. That is the kind of King he is.

I described to Chef Martin how *lechon* is roasted, and he was enthusiastic to do it. The male workers in the castle dug four pits at the far end of the castle grounds. I was glad I did not have to watch how they were butchered. After the pigs were ready for roasting, Chef Martin seasoned them, and I showed him how to stuff them with the leaves of the *tanglad* (lemon grass) to give them that special flavor and aroma. The men took turns in rotating the skewered pigs to ensure they cooked evenly over the live charcoal.

The King led us in saying grace before the meal. He announced that this thanksgiving dinner for the castle staff was my idea in appreciation of their service to the royal family. My King always credits me. They earlier hung lanterns to light up the *al fresco* dinner area. The roasted pigs were the main attraction during our Sunday dinner at the castle grounds. Ms. Ethel also served other dishes and desserts for all, but the *lechons* were the stars of the evening, and everybody discovered a delicacy from the Philippines. They all enjoyed eating especially the crispy skin.

Franco and I, with the rest of the royal family, mingled with the castle staff and shared their tables. I enjoyed conversing with the castle staff and knowing about their families and personal life. This is something I continue to imbibe from Franco, who has a big heart for all kinds of people. It was nice to see the castle staff having fun and enjoying the food with us.

"This is so good. *Squisito* (delicious)," Franco remarked while eating his *lechon* with a glass of beer. "Here, try this, darling." He got a piece of the crispy skin and put it into my mouth. The castle staff in our table who witnessed this smiled secretly. They probably found it sweet seeing their King feeding their Queen. It has become a habit with Franco to let me try something his taste buds approve of, and I find myself doing the same thing with him. Feeding each other can be something quite personal, and it comes off as a loving gesture too.

I showed Chef Martin how to cook the *lechon* leftovers, transforming them into another delicious Filipino dish called *paksiw*, which has the slightly sour taste from the vinegar. He liked it, and so did Franco. I finally satisfied my craving for this dish.

* * *

The hours that the King devotes to his grandkids are often valuable time where he imparts to them something, or teaches them a new lesson. Franco spent some time training Francesco on archery in the castle grounds. As he was doing that, I guided the girls to the kitchen to show them how to bake brownies, one of their favorite snacks. Olivia and Bianca were excited to learn, and I allowed them to measure and mix the ingredients themselves, transfer the mixture to the pans, and bake them in the oven. We chatted while waiting for the brownies to get done, and it was a pleasure listening to their stories about their school and friends. The brownies were a hit with the family. The girls were proud of their baking accomplishment. I was touched to hear them say, "*Nonna* taught us how to bake them," and I got a wink and a smile from Franco across the table.

Chapter

4

We finally devoted to Franco's book the time it deserved. He wrote the pages, and I edited whatever he finished. It was an ideal collaborative setup. He was now in the castle more days in a week, and I welcomed his presence. Some of my friends used to tell me that they are relieved when their husbands are out of the house because they can function better at home by themselves. It was quite the opposite with me because I love having Franco around all the time, and I do not tire of his presence. When we work together, we talk constantly, and share occasions of mirth and fun, so there is no room for boredom. We absolutely relish these precious times. Because we married late, we are still on our honeymoon stage, and that is what defines our union as special and fulfilling. I treasure every moment with him.

Every day I absorb gems of wisdom from my husband. He is a brilliant monarch, so interacting with him results in an endless learning journey, which consistently fuels my interests and enhances my knowledge storehouse, definitely adding luster to my role as Queen. I have become a better person because of him.

What I find incredible is he never makes me feel unimportant. He always respects my opinion. As King, he can easily disregard my views since I am merely from a third-world country, but he never makes me feel insignificant. Instead, he puts me on a pedestal, and values me as a person. He never hesitates to express his profound love for me, and that alone is my reason for loving him with equal intensity.

On one end of our bedroom is Franco's desk where he worked on the final pages of his book. He called out to me to check on the sentence he had just written on his laptop. As I approached his desk and bent down to read it, bringing our heads close, he surprised me with a kiss on the cheek.

"Darling, what are you doing?" I reacted with a smile.

"Why, can't I kiss my wife? You smell so good that I'm tempted to kiss you again." That is how pleasurable working with my King goes, and I appreciate it.

* * *

It was a busy month for the two of us in the final stages of the publication of Franco's book. He completed the closing page, and after my editing, the layout phase followed. He envisioned it from the start as a coffee-table book, which is larger in dimension than a regular book. Marvellans can proudly display it in their homes because it heralds their Kingdom's history and heritage. Franco wanted the book to instill a sense of belonging on the people of Marvella. We worked with the layout artist page by page in one of the rooms in the Palace. I assisted the layout artist in positioning the photos and organizing the text on the pages. I meticulously combed through the pages in its galley stage as its Editor.

Franco approved my suggested title:

Marvella:

A Miracle to Marvel at

It did sound appropriate, considering that it is what this Kingdom actually means. The book opened with:

Written by:

King Franco V

Edited by:

Queen Marianne I

The dedication on the succeeding page stated:

For the people of Marvella

On the next page after that was "**A Message from the King**" with this text:

"People of Marvella, this is our book. It has long been my dream to produce such a book, and for every Marvellan family to own a copy of it for the sole reason that I want all of you to know the rich history and heritage of our Kingdom. It chronicles the lives of our past monarchs, starting with King Franco I, my great great grandfather, and the relevant and interesting events marking those early years, leading up to the promising and victorious years of the present era. Our learnings are numerous. We are constantly driven by our insights and vision for the Kingdom, and it is what it is today because of all of you.

It is indeed providential that I met and married my Queen when I was conceptualizing this book. It brought our worlds together. She is an excellent Editor, and she was able to enhance this book significantly. It was her idea to generate the necessary funds to make its publication possible through some projects she initiated to free the monarchy of any monetary burden. I thank her for her initiative, collaboration, and most of all her love.

I share this book with all of you. The title itself is the very definition of 'Marvella.' Take great pride in being part of this Kingdom, which is our home."

Franco's signature appeared below. His reference to me again touched me.

On the page after that, occupying the entire page, was a photo version of our painting hanging at the castle. It was captioned: **King Franco V and Queen Marianne I of the Kingdom of Marvella.**

* * *

The coffee-table book had an impressive maroon-colored leather. The title, which was embossed in gold, was easily eye-catching. Below the bold title on the cover was the Marvellan flag, which appeared on the lower portion. Its flag is colorful. Horizontally, two-thirds of the right-hand portion is royal blue at the top and red at the lower portion. The monarchy's coat-of-arms in its colors occupied one-third of the left-hand portion against a white background.

The monarchy placed an initial order of 800,000 copies from the printer. It needed at least 625,000 copies for the families living in the Kingdom. Franco had no intention of making the book public, which explained the limited order. The monarchy agreed not to hold a formal book launching, but just a simple and quiet one at the museum since the book itself was a private endeavor.

It was a select crowd present during the cocktails. The book was well-received, and Franco and I were recipients of unceasing compliments. Word about the book spread around when the distribution of copies within the Kingdom was in full swing, and some outsiders got wind of it. It was featured in a local magazine, and neighboring countries picked up the story. The Palace received several queries about its availability. After consulting the King, the Palace placed an additional order, bringing the total to a million copies. Franco and I harbored no doubts that the book would reach unbelievable heights in readership. This was his legacy to the people of Marvella. A permanent smile registered on his face for the next days after its resounding success. Seeing Franco this happy was contagious, and it rubbed on me, so I was happy too.

* * *

"Darling, I feel great right now. Let's return to Positano and retrace the happy moments we spent there. It will be purely our 'we' time," Franco suggested from out of the blue.

"I'd like that very much." Remembering the ecstasy I experienced in Positano on our honeymoon filled me with much anticipation and excitement.

We arrived in Positano late afternoon. We checked into the same suite we occupied before, just on time to catch the transcendent beauty of the incredible sunset from the balcony. For us, it was undoubtedly a romantic scene with Franco enfolding me in his embrace. The sun gradually descended and faded into the horizon majestically, bidding goodbye to the day, and the surrounding area was bathed in a golden hue. He gently turned me to face him. He tilted my chin and gazed down at me, compelling me to look directly into his eyes. I could not evade those deep-blue eyes, which held me spell-bound and warmed my very core. He kissed me passionately, then enclosed me in a bear hug, and I remained locked in his arms.

"Darling, I want to stay here forever," I said to him.

"In Positano? Not Marvella?"

"In your arms." He gave out a chuckle as he released me from his embrace, but still holding me close to him, and looking intently at me with an expression replete with unleashed emotions.

"My love, I will never let you go. When you came into my life, my entire world changed. My love for you is so powerful that it knows no bounds. I can't be any happier than this being with you. As King, I have received countless blessings in my life, but you are my greatest blessing. I promise to love you until infinity."

"Oh, Franco, my love for you is immeasurable. It is timeless. You're the only man I ever loved."

"My love, my wife, and my Queen. You are my Forever, and I will always love you far beyond that."

-The End-

About the Author

Cristina Monro is a penname this Filipino author uses when writing fiction. This is her third romance fiction. She also published two other books in the nonfiction genre. She is an editor, English instructor, and an oil and acrylic artist. She has a post-graduate Diploma in Language and Literacy Education from the University of the Philippines, a Bachelor of Arts degree (English major) from Xavier University-Ateneo de Cagayan, a Certificate of Teaching English as a Second/Foreign Language from De La Salle University, and Associate in Secretarial from Maryknoll College. She received a Fellowship Grant from the US-Asia Environmental Partnership and completed the Program for Development Managers at the Asian Institute of Management.

* * *